COSTUME SHOP

III

By

Bobby Legend

COSTUME SHOP III

Published through Legend Publishing Company

INTRODUCTION

The mystery of the Costume Shop continues. Every year, during and around Halloween, people were disappearing at an alarming rate. The police were baffled by their peers and others disappearing, and no suspects to question. With the disappearance of four of their detectives and a well-known senator, the local police department wanted to find an answer to this mystery and find it quickly. In the meantime, the powers that be were inundated with phone calls from worried wives and husbands about missing loved ones. Finally, one person stepped up to the plate: His quest: to find an answer to the Legend of Hollow Pass.

CHAPTER 1

It had been nearly six years since Detective John Matthew had disappeared. Since then, the investigation of his disappearance and that of three other detectives out of the same local police department had been shut down and hadn't been replaced by a new investigator.

As Jack Matthew, son of Detective Jonathon Matthew, sat watching television, a news report came on talking about people missing in the area.

"And now," said the reporter, "Fox News wants to say a few words about the disappearances of more than twenty people in this area that goes back to more than two decades. Some say it is a serial killer that's taking these people and doing god knows what. Others say it is the Legend of Hollow Pass. Fox News has no opinion, only that these disappearances always happen about ten days before and right up to Halloween. Will it ever stop? Senator Bailey, Detective Charles Webber, Detective Brad Zoolu, Detective Jonathon Matthew, Detective Johnson Waters and many others, to just name a few. The powers that be can't let this continue. We must have an answer of what happened to these people. And that is the Fox News Opinion. We would like to know what you, our television viewers think? Phone or text to: Fox News Opinion Poll. Thank You. And I'm reporter John Rodgers, wishing you and yours a goodnight."

When Jack Matthew saw and heard this news report a lightbulb went off in his head. He had just received his PHD in Psychology and studied Exorcism at the Vatican in Rome. But came back to the States when he was suspended and placed on probation for alcoholism. So now, for the time being, he was on a Sabbatical. He decided, while wrestling with his disease and conscious, and with a lot of time on his hands, to investigate these rash of disappearances, as his father once had. He would start by making a profile of the serial killer some thought might behind this. Secondly, he'd investigate the Legend of Hollow Pass to see if this superstition or rumor had any validity and could stand up to real evidence. But first he must get the okay from his Bishop and church.

Jack sat for a long time thinking about his dad. He really missed him; and to disappear like he did. Everyone had told him that his dad had left the state with a younger woman. But Jack didn't believe that. He knew his dad better than anyone. He knew that something "bad" had happened to him. It was his father who had pointed Jack towards the priesthood. As he reminisced about all the good and fun times he had with his dad…that thought made him want to investigate his dad's disappearance immediately. From that, he hoped it would lead to answers to the disappearances of others. Were they dead or still alive? That thought raced through is mind as he lay in bed, as well as others, especially about how to proceed with the investigation. Even though he wasn't a detective like his father had been, he still had great investigative skills and instincts due to his psychological background.

Jack decided that he needed to speak with his father's boss, Captain Bird for an update and to hopefully pick up any files and reports on his father's investigation. Then, he would have to track down any of the witnesses that his father may have interviewed. And to do that he would have to visit his dad's vacant house to see if he had left behind any evidence, such as tapes or papers or anything of importance that would help in the investigation.

***

The following morning, Jack readied to leave for the meeting with Captain Bird. However, he was still fighting his demons; to settle his nerves he had a couple of shots of whiskey before driving to the station. He had been slowly weening himself from his disease and had come a long way, but still had a long road to tow.

During his drive, the weather had turned bleak and foul. Dark clouds, thunder, lightning, heavy rain and fog filled the air. Visibility was terrible. It was practically impossible to see the taillights of the car directly ahead.

The cars had slowed to a near trickle due to the nasty weather. But suddenly, traffic jammed to a halt. Nobody could really see the reason behind the traffic jam. So after nearly five minutes of not moving, Jack took the key out of the ignition and hopped out of his vehicle, then proceeded to walk up the street hoping to find the cause of the tie-up.

Just thirty feet ahead, a crowd gathered in the middle of the street. As Jack broke through the crowd to get a good look at the holdup, he was surprised to see an elderly lady, kneeling, crying hysterically, and speaking incomprehensibly.

As the rain poured down, no one in the crowd put out a hand to help the old woman, so Jack went over to her, put his windbreaker over her clothes, which he noticed was some type of costume, and after showing the woman his identification, introduced himself as Father Matthew, which seemed to have a calming effect on the woman. But her words were still incomprehensible and her crying continued. He grabbed her arm and helped her to her feet, and then walked her back to his car and placed her in the passenger seat, then he got behind the wheel and continued on his way to his meeting with Captain Bird. That was the only thing he could think of at that moment that was beneficial to himself and his passenger. She gave out no information that would help Matthew help her. So he figured who else but the police to investigate the old woman and how she ended up in the middle of a main thoroughfare in the middle of the city wearing what seemed to be, a Halloween costume.

Twelve minutes later, he had gotten the woman out of the car and into the station. She was still weeping as Father Matthew handed her over to the Desk Sergeant, Officer Marilyn Campbell. After wishing the woman well he proceeded to Captain Bird's office with the help from a janitor.

Bird saw a man that looked familiar at his office door and invited him in.

"Captain Bird, I'm Jack Matthew. It's been a long time since we last met."

The two men shook hands. The Captain thought he smelled alcohol on Matthew's breath and asked him if he had been drinking so early in the morning.

"Jack, have you been drinking? I can smell alcohol on your breath."

Jack didn't know what to say and lied. "It must be my cheap cologne." And left it at that.

"Whew," Bird exclaimed. "I'd invest in some better smelling cologne."

As the two took their seats, Bird couldn't get over how much the kid looked like his father.

"Jack, you look so much like your father, it's unbelievable."

"Thank you, sir." He smiled.

"Geez, the last time I saw you," Bird recalled, "you were on your way to Europe."

Matthew nodded. "Yes," he replied. "I went to study at the Vatican in Rome."

Bird scratched his head and asked him what he did there?

"Well, I received my PHD in Psychology and studied exorcism after becoming a priest."

Bird sat up in his seat when he heard the word priest. "Oh, I'm sorry, Father," he said apologetically. "I couldn't tell. You're not wearing your collar."

"You're correct. I'm actually on a well-needed vacation. A kind of Sabbatical. So I'm really not allowed to wear it. Although, I do at times for a calming effect."

Bird smiled and asked, "So what's on your mind, Jack?"

"Well, sir. I know my dad's investigation was shut down soon after he disappeared, but I was hoping that you could give me an update, if there is any, and possibly any files or records from that investigation."

"Why? Why do you want the files?"

Jack looked down at the floor and answered, "I'm going to investigate my dad's disappearance."

Bird seemed perplexed by Matthew's answer.

Matthew continued. "I know your investigators concluded that my dad left the state and started a new life with a younger woman. But I don't buy that."

Bird looked confused. "Well, we never found a body," he answered.

Matthew leaned forward in his seat and told Bird the best reason for his thinking. "Even if my dad did what you say, he still would have contacted his children. No, Captain

Bird, I believe he was either murdered, as the TV commentator suggested or his disappearance has something to do with the Legend of Hollow Pass."

"What do you think, Captain. Do you believe in this legend, this legend called Hollow Pass?"

"Superstitious nonsense," he replied sarcastically. "It doesn't exist!"

Matthew smiled. "I guess I agree with you about that. Even though I don't know too much about it, only what I heard on television. I will have to visit the library and see what they have on the subject."

An officer came into the room and wanted to speak with Bird privately.

Matthew got the hint and stood up to leave.

"In the meantime," Bird told Matthew, "I'll track down any files or reports that we have on your dad…and if you give me your number I'll call you to pick them up."

Matthew nodded and quickly wrote his telephone number on a piece of paper and handed it to Bird.

"Good," said Bird as he stood and shook Matthew's hand.

"It was good seeing you again, Captain." Matthew turned and left the room.

Before leaving the station, Matthew asked Desk Sergeant Campbell about the old woman.

"We had to take her to the hospital," she answered.

Matthew looked concerned.

"Not to worry, Sir. She's being well taken care of. But I gotta tell ya… that woman was a little Coo, Coo!"

Matthew smiled and thanked her, then left the station. Driving home he debated his next plan of action. He decided to have some breakfast before going to the hospital to see the elderly woman that he had helped and possibly saved from doing harm to herself. He suddenly changed his mind and decided breakfast could wait for an hour or so. He wanted to see how the old woman was doing and see if she was coherent or still in a psychotic state.

***

Arriving at the hospital, Matthew was told that the elderly woman in question was taken from the hospital to the local mental facility for raving lunatics.

"She was calm when they first brought her in," said the nurse, "but soon after she was an incoherent raving lunatic. It took five people to hold her down; a woman that is in her late seventies, one hundred and ten pounds, and not a millimeter over five-feet, two inches. She was a handful to say the least. We were able to inject her with three hundred milligrams of Thorazine, and even with all that in her system, it barely made a dent. So we had to call the mental institution and they came and picked her up."

Matthew asked her if the woman had left anything of importance behind that might give them an inkling of her name.

"The only stuff that was left here was the clothes she was wearing. I think it's a costume."

The nurse went behind the nurses' counter and grabbed the bag full of clothes and set them on top of the counter.

"Can I take them with me? I'll take full responsibility." He showed her his identification that showed he was a Catholic priest. "I'll return them to her when I visit her. I want to see how she's doing."

"I guess it's alright." She handed him the bag of clothes.

Matthew thanked her and again promised to return them to their rightful owner.

He left the hospital and decided to finally eat breakfast before setting out for the mental institution. He decided to eat at Gabriele's Hoagie Shop, the same place his dad and other detectives congregated to have drinks and their famous steak and cheese hoagies.

However, a steak and cheese hoagie wasn't on Matthew's mind; instead he ordered a steak, eggs, and cheese hoagie.

The waitress brought Matthew his order, and as she set his water glass and the plate onto the table, stared intently into his face.

Matthew noticed her staring and asked, "Can I help you, Miss?"

She finally snapped out of it, as if she was daydreaming and replied, "Oh, I'm sorry. I didn't mean to stare, but you remind me of someone. I just can't put a finger on it."

"Do I?"

She stood silent, thinking. "Do you come here often?"

He told her it was his first time. "But my dad used to come in here quite often years back."

"Oh, yeah, who is your dad? Maybe I know him."

Matthew nodded and answered, "You might have met him. He came in here with another Detective, Brad Zoolu. Did you know him?"

"Of course. But I heard he left his job and the state for a woman."

"That's what they said. They also said that of my dad."

"So what's your dad's name?"

"Detective John Matthew. Did you know him?"

She thought for a few long seconds and exclaimed, "Yeah! Yeah! Now I know who you're speaking about. He came in here with Detective Zoolu quite often."

Matthew smiled and began to eat his hoagie.

Her eyes lit up. "Now I see the resemblance," she added, smiling. "You are the spitting image of your father." She turned and walked back behind the counter.

After finishing his meal, Matthew paid his bill and as he was exiting the front door, a uniformed police officer met him and introduced himself.

"I'm Officer Mark Law. You are Father Matthew, aren't you?" the cop asked him.

"Yes. Yes, sir. What's the problem?"

The cop told Matthew the reason for the visit. "Captain Bird told me to find you. He needs to speak with you on an important matter."

"How in the heck did you find me?" Matthew asked the cop, perplexed by the possibility that he was being followed for some reason.

"Well, we knew you had to eat breakfast and might possibly visit your dad's old stomping ground. So I thought I'd check. I guess I got lucky!"

"Boy, I guess you did," Matthew replied, as they walked back to their cars. "This is the very first time I came here since I was a kid. You must be some kind of psychic."

Matthew for some reason had a feeling of distrust from the cop. He couldn't put a finger on it, but finding him at Gabriele's, he was sure, wasn't coincidental.

"I'll follow you back to the station," Law told Matthew just before he got into his cop car.

Matthew again felt uncomfortable with this whole situation. He didn't need to be *followed* to the police station. "I can get their all by myself," he thought to himself.

And Matthew was right. Ten minutes after leaving the restaurant parking lot, he was standing in Captain Bird's office wondering why he had been summoned there. He suddenly noticed that he wasn't the only visitor. There were also two rather gorgeous females sitting in the room.

Matthew spoke up first. "What am I doing here?" he asked Bird, who was sitting at his desk.

"Father Matthew, I asked you here for a couple of reasons," he answered. "And two of those reasons are sitting next to you." He pointed at the two women.

Matthew nodded to the women.

Bird continued. "The lady closest to you, Father, is Amy Strang, daughter to State Senator Arnold Strang. And the lady next to her is Detective Carolyn Hampton. She's been temporarily transferred from Missing Persons to my department."

"Okay, but what's this have to do with me," Matthew asked him.

Before answering, Bird picked his teeth with a worn toothpick and then told Matthew that State Senator Strang and his wife, Mildred, were missing and Detective Hampton was investigating their disappearances. "The FBI are also investigating but we are not working in unison with them. It seems they can do without our help. And you, Father, are investigating your father's disappearance. I thought that maybe you and Miss Hampton could help each other by keeping each other informed concerning your investigations. Maybe you two can come up with an answer for these disappearances. For some reason, around this time of year, people disappear into thin air."

"And my parents are two of the people," Strang acknowledged. "Both my mom and dad were going to a costume shop to get costumes for the Policemen's Halloween Ball that's coming up. They never came back. I'm afraid that they've been killed. Or taken."

"Taken?" Matthew asked her.

"Yes. You know. The Legend of Hollow Pass," Strang answered nervously.

"Come on now, Amy," Bird said angrily. "The Legend of Hollow Pass is a story made up to sell newspapers. It's pure superstition."

"I'm sorry, Captain Bird," retorted Strang, "but I can't discount that theory. Many scholars believe in the Legend. And they don't work for any newspaper!"

"Well now," Bird said, apologetically, "let's not have any more of that kind of talk in my office. We'll find your mom and dad. I promise you."

"I hope so," whined Strang.

Matthew stood to leave and told Bird he had business to take care of. "Well Captain, if that's it, I have things to do and I need to get them done sooner rather than later."

"Before you go, take this with you." Bird handed Matthew a manila envelope containing the file on his father's investigation. "I hope it helps in your endeavor."

"Thank you, Captain Bird."

The two shook hands. Matthew turned to leave but then remembered he needed to exchange telephone numbers with Detective Hampton, so they exchanged business cards.

A few minutes later, Matthew was back on the road driving again in hellish weather, although the rain had died down for the moment to a light sprinkle. He returned home before visiting the mental hospital. He wanted to look over the file on his dad's investigation, while having a shot or two of whiskey to calm his nerves.

The first thing Matthew did when he entered his home was to grab his bottle of whiskey and a shot glass, then filled the glass to the brim. He gulped it down and then poured another, which he gulped down as well. He sat down at the kitchen table and opened up the manila envelope Captain Bird had given him.

Matthew was surprised to see just one page of information with much of it redacted. "Why," he wondered.

There were a number of names mentioned, like the FBI but next to that word, everything, about a paragraph was redacted. It also had the name of Samantha Polk; and next to her name was a redacted word. But over it was written: reporter. Bobby Legend was another; next to his name was also the word: reporter; next to that was the word: journal.

Matthew had heard the name Samantha Polk from his dad in a letter concerning the investigation of the disappearance of his partner, Brad Zoolu, which was exactly two years before his father's. He hadn't heard the name Bobby Legend before, nor did he know what the word "journal" had to do with his dad's investigation. But he was going to find out.

The words, Costume Shop and Serial Killer were also mentioned. But whatever was written on those subjects had also been redacted—more than two paragraphs of information.

The last statement made on the page was a summation that John Matthew and Samantha Polk left their families to start a new life elsewhere. The page ended with two words: "Case closed!"

Matthew wondered why Captain Bird had given him this file on his dad's investigation. There was very little pertinent information that wasn't redacted about his dad's disappearance. What was so classified that the ***powers that be*** redacted large parts of the information? What were they trying to hide and why? These questions and others were running through Matthew's head.

Matthew pondered the situation and his next step in the investigation while pouring himself another shot of whiskey. After downing that and a few others, he decided to visit his dad's house that had been sitting empty since his disappearance.

Before leaving the house, he had to have an additional shot of whiskey to help him deal with the memories of years gone by. Matthew knew he shouldn't drink and drive but he had been doing it for so many years and without repercussions. This was the main reason he was suspended from the Vatican and put on Sabbatical. But he still got behind the wheel of his car and drove to the basically abandoned dwelling his family had once lived in.

Entering the home brought back pent up feelings of loving memories. He shut the front door and then walked into the living room and sat down on the dusty couch to catch his breath. He took a quick look around, taking in the surroundings. Everything had been left intact, even though it had been searched many years ago during the investigation into his father's disappearance. Other than a thick coating of dust and a few spider webs in the corners of the walls, the interior of the house looked the same as it had during Matthew's teen years. So, he was hoping there would be something, some kind of evidence that the investigative team had overlooked that might point him in the right direction. But the investigators had gone through the house with a fine-tooth comb. They were very thorough because after looking under the rugs, in closets, going through the dressers Matthew couldn't find anything of pertinent value, except one little piece of cardboard with the number fifteen East—two hours, written on it. (15 East—two hours.) He didn't know what it meant or if it was even related to his father's disappearance but he kept it anyways and placed the piece of cardboard in his pocket.

Before leaving, he took another look around, remembering how happy he had been growing up in the house. He hoped that one day soon the house would again be full of life and laughter, preferably from his father. And Matthew would do everything in his power to bring him home. Alive!

Once he locked the front door, he returned to his home to think about the next steps in his investigation. But first, he remembered about the old woman.

After having a couple of shots of whiskey, he decided that in the morning he would visit her to see how she was doing and also bring her the clothes that were left behind at the hospital. Afterwards, Matthew wanted to visit Captain Bird and ask him about the file, or lack, there of; and why all the redacting?

Matthew spent the rest of the day drinking and thinking. He also spent time on the Internet trying to find out exactly who this Bobby Legend was and the importance of his journal. As the night grew near, the bottle of whiskey lay empty. He returned to the kitchen to retrieve another bottle. He grabbed it and the bag of clothes the woman had worn. He was anxious to see them, hoping to see a name or something that he, the police and hospital officials had overlooked.

Matthew checked them inside and out with a fine tooth comb but came up empty-handed. Although, he had never seen such a costume as this; it seemed to be a dress for a Cheyenne Indian squaw. The beadwork was exquisite on a hide, an animal hide of some sort, maybe deer or elk that was extremely weather-worn. The leather and beadwork looked like it had been hand-sewn more than a hundred years before. He wondered what costume shop would rent out costumes of museum quality. Matthew folded up the costume and placed it back into the bag.

The sun had gone down hours ago and Father Matthew had a little too much to drink. But he was used to it. His sobriety wasn't an issue for him at the moment. Sleep was. As soon as his head hit the pillow, the snoring began. He was sound asleep within seconds.

CHAPTER 2

The following morning, Matthew awoke with a hangover. Another feeling he was used to. He had a quick fix for his problem. He poured himself a shot of whiskey for breakfast, which washed the phlegm from his throat and stopped his "shakes". But one wasn't enough. He poured himself two more before leaving for the mental hospital with costume in hand. He also took with him the file to return to Captain Bird.

As Matthew was driving along, he reached into his jacket pocket and pulled out the piece of cardboard that he had found at his father's house the day before. He looked again at the number fifteen (15) and the words "East—2hrs. He now believed it could possibly be a road, with the 1 being a capitol I instead. Matthew then remembered that Interstate I-5 was not too far away. He thought, maybe it meant to "Go East on Interstate I-5 for two hours. But then what? What happens then?" He didn't know if this little bit of information had anything to do with his father's investigation but he would look into it and travel the road for that length of time. He figured that maybe he would see something familiar or maybe find that costume shop that was mentioned in the file. Or maybe find nothing!

Matthew finally reached the hospital without mishap, and parked his car. As he walked the five hundred feet to the front entrance, and while holding the bag of clothes under his arm, he put on his collar hoping it would have a calming effect on the old woman. But looking at the old prison-like hospital, in the shape of an old gothic castle with monstrous gargoyles overlooking the grounds to ward off evil spirits gave him an **unnerving** effect; it gave him the **willies**. The trees overlooking the grounds seemed to envelope one's body, stalking, staring and watching your every move. He was relieved when he finally entered the hollow and nearly empty building. He suddenly stopped in his tracks. The dirty gray walls along with the many missing floor tiles, and the decaying furniture made the place look unsanitary.

Matthew just shook his head in shame as he gave the place the "once over." Looking at the many tiers and heavy metal doors to keep their patients safely locked in their rooms, the place, he noticed, was set up more like a prison than a hospital. The screams and cries echoed throughout the empty building. He couldn't take much more of the madness especially with the hangover he was carrying. So he walked quickly across the way to the front desk.

Matthew showed his identification to the nurse behind the desk and asked for her help. "Ma'am," he said, as he placed the bag of clothes onto the desk, "an elderly woman was picked up at General Hospital yesterday and brought here. She was in a state of shock and completely incoherent when taken to the hospital and had no identification on her. Do you know who I'm talking about?"

She told Matthew that two unidentified elderly and incoherent women had been transported to their facility the day before.

"Of course, they were incoherent, Father," she told him, "because both were given three hundred milligrams of Thorazine before being transported so they've been pretty well out of it since."

She added that both had been labeled as Jane Does. So Matthew had two choices.

"I'm sorry, I introduced myself, but I didn't get your name," Matthew told her.

"Oh, forgive me, Father. I'm nurse Brachit."

Matthew let out a little laugh. "You were that nurse in that Jack Nicolson movie."

She noticed that Matthew seemed a little unstable. "Father, have you been drinking?" She placed her nose close to his face and smelled alcohol on his breath. "You *have* been drinking!"

He lied and told her it was his cologne that she smelled, not alcohol.

The nurse gave Matthew a quizzical look and decided to give him the benefit of the doubt for the simple fact that he was a priest.

The nurse agreed to help him out. So, she, along with two big and burly orderlies walked with Matthew up four flights of stairs to the room of the first Jane Doe. An orderly pounded on the door to get the woman's attention. But it did no good. She just stared at the floor.

Matthew looked through the six-inch square window on the door but couldn't tell if it was the same woman, because she was kneeling on the floor, in a straightjacket and her hair was covering her face. The nurse unlocked the door and allowed Father Matthew to enter the padded room but not before the orderlies. They stood guard just in case *things* got out of hand.

Matthew tried to get the woman's attention by speaking softly to her, but she wouldn't look up, so he took it upon himself and lifted her face towards his and saw that it wasn't the woman he was looking for but noticed this woman had a very bruised and battered face. He turned to tell his findings to the nurse but she was quick to reply.

"She did it to herself," the nurse acknowledged, "that's why we had to put her into a straightjacket."

Matthew didn't buy her quick answer and told her so. "The woman didn't give herself two black eyes and a swollen forehead. You better see to it that she gets some medical attention."

The nurse didn't say a word and Matthew figured he had said enough and left it at that. He didn't want her angry at him, especially after seeing that this woman was not the one he was looking for.

The group left that room and headed down the hall to the padded room where the other elderly woman was residing. When they reached the room, Matthew again looked through the door's small window to see if he could recognize the woman. But this woman too was kneeling on the dirty floor, and was also wrapped in a straightjacket. Her hair too, was covering her face, which made it difficult to recognize her. As the door opened, the woman looked up in a dazed and confused manner.

As Matthew and company entered the room, the woman tried speaking but her words were indistinguishable. She drooled as she spoke incoherent words that sounded like she was speaking in "tongues."

But Matthew had found the woman that he had been looking for. Although, she still looked in very bad shape and it seemed was still in a state of shock.

"Do you know who this lady is yet?" Matthew asked the nurse.

The nurse shook her head. "No," she replied. "She had no identification on her...and her fingerprints, we were told, were not in any data base as far as we know. That's why she's still a 'Jane Doe.'"

Matthew asked the nurse to return the woman's clothes to her that he had placed on the front desk.

"I will be back tomorrow to check on the woman. I need to know who she is. I am the one responsible for her being here."

"What do you mean by that, Father?" asked Nurse Brachit.

"I was the one who found her in the middle of the street and took her to the police station, who took her to City Hospital. Then you guys got her."

The nurse let out a sigh, then said, "Well, evidently, this is the right place for her...for the time being."

With that said, the group turned and left the room, leaving the poor lady alone and in disarray. Matthew felt sorry for her but there was nothing he could do, but pray for her safety and sanity. He would definitely check in on her again to see how she was doing and if there were any changes in her demeanor.

Before leaving the facility, Matthew thanked Nurse Brachit and the orderlies for their time and told them he would return bright and early the following morning.

He drove away from that facility a little disheartened and a little shaken. But he had seen worse during his exorcism training for the Vatican. Many of the people inhabited by demons were in much worse shape. But seeing those two old women nearly catatonic and prisoners not only of the hospital but also prisoners in their own minds reminded him of past exorcisms, which was a very big reason he fell into drink. He only hoped that they would come out of their stupor sooner rather than later.

***

Matthew had planned to drive directly from the nut house to the station but after twenty minutes in that crazy place brought back many bad memories. So before confronting Captain Bird, he decided to return home and pour himself some instant courage...which he did, and finished nearly a half bottle of whiskey before making the ten-minute drive to the station.

Matthew walked slowly and deliberately, trying not to stagger, to Bird's office. As he entered the room, he noticed those same two women that were there the day before sitting across from the Captain.

Bird motioned Matthew to "pull up a chair."

Matthew did as ordered, and being as drunk as he was, plopped his behind into the seat, nearly toppling over.

Bird noticed and asked Matthew if he was okay. "Are you alright, Father?"

Matthew nodded.

Bird continued. "You remember Miss Strang and Miss Hampton, don't you?" he asked Matthew.

Again, Matthew didn't speak but nodded as he looked at them.

"I'm glad you stopped by, Father," Bird acknowledged. "I have something important to speak with you about. But first, what did you want to see me about?"

Matthew placed the manila envelope on his desk containing the nearly one page of redacted material. "I just wanted to give this back. All the important information has been redacted. I don't know why you even gave me this."

Bird shrugged and told Matthew he had given him everything that was on file. "I'm sorry, that's all we had."

"But what was so confidential that the ***powers that be*** had to redact nearly everything on the page?"

"I'll look into it," Bird promised. "We'll talk about that at a later date. Right now, I need to ask a favor of you."

"What do you need?" answered Matthew.

"I need you and Hampton to fly to Chicago and interview a suspect about the Senator's disappearance and possibly your father's."

"My father's?" exclaimed Matthew. "What does he have to do with my father's disappearance?"

Bird explained that the suspect was in the area during both men's disappearances. "We can put him here six years ago, and we can put him here yesterday. I figured seeing that you have your PHD in Psychology and you are investigating your dad's disappearance, you might want to be in on the questioning and just read his overall persona, then give us a profile."

But Matthew seemed hesitant to travel and made the excuse that he was afraid of flying, adding, "And I'm not a cop!"

"Listen, Father," Bird replied. "Your dad was a very good friend of mine. And I just thought you could help us and help yourself. Kind of like killing two birds with one stone, so to speak."

"I don't know, Captain."

"Look, it's only three or four hours of your time and it will give you something to do besides drink," Bird said, bluntly.

Matthew sighed.

Hampton joined the conversation. "Come on, Father. It'll be fun," she assured him. "Who knows, we may just find the person that may be complicit in many of these missing people. What do you say, Father?" She gave him a big smile and a wink.

The two were close in age, both in their mid-thirties. She had the looks and body of a model. Matthew had a full head of beautiful blond hair, nearly six feet, two inches tall and nearly two hundred pounds of raw muscle. But being suspended from the Church and on a Sabbatical, he wasn't working out as much and definitely wasn't working on his problem with alcohol. He tried to decline the offer.

He shrugged his shoulders and whined, "But I don't like flying!"

"But we sure could use your help," Bird pleaded. "And it's only for a half-day at the most. What do you say, Father? Will you tag along with Carolyn?"

Matthew looked at Hampton and nodded. "Yeah, Okay. But just for a few hours."

Hampton gave him another big smile.

Captain Bird ended the meeting by telling Matthew the time of the flight. "Be here by four this afternoon and I'll have you and Carolyn driven to the airport."

Matthew nodded then stood to leave but before leaving Bird gave him some advice.

"And Father, get yourself lots of hot coffee. I think you could use it!"

Matthew nodded. "I'll see you at four." He turned and left Bird's office and headed for home.

He returned home all right, but not to drink hot coffee. Matthew wanted more "courage" before he boarded that plane. He was deathly afraid of flying, and when he had to leave Rome for the United States, he took a cruise ship home. Flying just wasn't his "cup of tea."

Matthew had a few hours to kill, so he made the most of it exercising his arm. He drank four shots before drinking directly from the bottle. By the time he had to leave for the station, he had finished the nearly half bottle of whiskey. But he could hide his drunkenness well; just not the smell. So, to hide that, he doused his clothes with a strong-smelling cologne.

While looking into the bathroom mirror he noticed that he still had his "collar" on. He began taking it off and then thought better of it. "Maybe it will help during the interview if the suspect knows I'm a priest and not a cop," he thought to himself, and then buttoned his collar.

***

It was nearly four o'clock by the time Matthew arrived at the station. He was met at the door by Hampton...and the limo driver that was driving them to the airport. As soon as the two got into the back seat of the limo, Hampton could smell the powerful cologne that Matthew had sloshed on all over his clothes.

"Damn, Father," she said sniffing the air. "Do you think you have enough cologne on?" She went on, adding, "And damn if that ain't the awfullest smelling cologne I have ever smelled. Whew!"

"I'm sorry about that," Matthew answered. "I guess I did put on a little bit heavy."

"I guess you did," Hampton retorted.

They both laughed.

Once they had reached the airport, they still had plenty of time before boarding so they decided to visit a dimly lit bar to have a drink and relax during their free time. They each ordered drinks: Hampton, a Pina Colada and Matthew, two double shots of whiskey. He chugged the first one, and then just as fast, the second. Hampton couldn't believe it. Matthew drank his drinks so fast that he had emptied both glasses in the time it took her to blink. He then ordered two more doubles. Hampton couldn't believe her eyes. She was sitting with a priest who was an "alky!" She watched as he chugged another two shots of whiskey and then asked him about it.

"You're knocking them back pretty quick there, aren't you, Father?"

"I'm fine. Just a little fearful of flying."

"Can't you just ask god to protect you?" she asked, smiling.

"I do," he replied. "But if he will or not, that's up to him."

They both laughed.

She looked him deep in his eyes and said, "You know, if you weren't a priest I think I could go for a guy like you."

Matthew's face turned a deep red. Even though it was dark in the bar, the candle lit table proved his embarrassment.

Hampton looked at her watch and told Matthew it was time to leave. After paying their bill, the two boarded the plane to Chicago. From takeoff to landing, Hampton held onto Matthew's hand during the short flight, trying to keep him calm, especially when he found out that they weren't serving alcoholic beverages.

They arrived none too soon for Father Matthew and went directly to city jail where they met with an apologetic Detective Jerry Firby.

"I'm sorry," Firby told them, "but there's been a little problem. It seems our suspect tried to play tough guy and assaulted one of our detectives, so some of our boys disciplined him and put him in the hospital. But he should be out by the morning. In fact, he will be out by morning. I'll see to that and then you'll be able to question him. Say, eight o'clock tomorrow morning."

The two out-of-towners were shocked at the news and weren't prepared for an overnight stay. Worse than that, there was a convention in town and rooms were unavailable, except for a cheap downtown motel that had only one room available, and with only a double bed. After two hours, and more than twenty phone calls to as many hotels and motels in a twenty-mile radius, they decided to make do with the one bed room. At least they had a liquor store just fifty feet away and a nice restaurant/disco next to it.

The couple were disappointed with their surroundings but they were professionals and adults and became better friends as the minutes passed.

After checking into their room, Matthew took off his collar and placed it into his jacket pocket and then unbuttoned his shirt.

After washing up, and fixing their hair the two walked over to the restaurant and had a decent steak dinner, and afterwards, went across the way and sat in the disco.

They listened to music while ordering drinks. But soon after, the music stopped and the conversation began. Matthew and Hampton talked mostly about themselves and downed their first drinks within minutes and ordered more.

The conversation switched to their suspect and the questions they would ask him.

But after their third round of drinks a song came on that Hampton was wild about and asked Matthew to dance. He hesitantly obliged and slow danced with her on the dance floor. She wrapped her arms around his body and pressed her body against his while placing his hand lower and lower down her back until it rested on her butt. By the end of the song, Hampton looked up at him, placed her hand behind his head and lowered it until their lips meant. Seconds later, both realized what had just happened and broke their hold on one another and returned to their seats for another drink before retiring to their room. They walked hand in hand going from the restaurant to the room, with Hampton's head resting on Matthew's shoulder. They were feeling **no pain** and acting like two school kids on their first blind date. But as soon as they entered the room, Matthew realized that he was still a priest and he would be breaking his vows to the church if it went any further than an innocent kiss or two. So, he tried to change the atmosphere by making conversation. But first, they each washed up, changed out of their clothes and into their bathrobes, which the motel provided to each customer. Matthew turned on the television and then both lay on the bed, very close to one another with Hampton's head resting on his chest.

Matthew asked her about the subject of the Legend of Hollow Pass. "You know, I didn't hear your opinion on the Hollow Pass Legend. Is there any justification to the rumors that spirits are taking these people to La-La land?"

At first, Hampton didn't want to talk about it. But with a little pleading from Matthew she relented. "I'm not sure if I believe it or not," she acknowledged. "But something's going on during those two weeks before Halloween. I mean ninety percent of the people that end up missing, disappears during those two weeks. So, it does seem that the Legend does have some merit. But if I had to choose between a serial killer and the Legend of Hollow Pass, I think I would have to pick the serial killer."

"Good choice," Matthew exclaimed. "Even though I've seen some crazy things during my exorcism training, it's still hard for me to believe in the Legend."

Hampton sat up. "Exorcism!" she barked. "You exorcise demons from sick people and don't believe in the Legend? *Incredible*!"

"That's true," he told her, as she rested her head once again on his chest.

"Let me get this straight, Father."

"Call me, Jack."

"Okay, Jack. You believe in god, who you've never met and only know him through the Bible. You, yourself just admitted that you exorcise demons and spirits from people in need. So why can't it be the spirits that are taking these people, who, by coincidence, we found out, were descendants of the townspeople who massacred not only all the medicine men of the tribe but also all the women and children. Nobody was left alive. The bodies mutilated and chopped up. And before the Indians were killed, some of the tribesmen cursed the killers and their town. Soon after, the townspeople died from the plague. Because those Indians weren't given an Indian burial and taken to the spirit world of their great, great grandfather's grandfathers, those Indian spirits have been taking those descendants in place of those Indians that were massacred, to allow the murdered Indians a place in the afterlife. That's the Legend of Hollow Pass."

"Wow, what a story. That's one for the ages."

Not too much was said after that. Soon after, they were fast asleep and out like a light.

***

At six-thirty the next morning, the phone rang. It was the desk calling for a wakeup call. Both out-of-towners hearing the ringing, woke up simultaneously, which gave them more than an hour to kill before leaving for the city jail.

They washed, dressed and then waited for the taxi to arrive. While waiting for the ride, Matthew walked quickly to the liquor store and purchased four one ounce bottles of whiskey, enough for four good shots. Seconds after paying for them, he drank all four bottles before leaving the store. Soon after, he returned to his room and waited for the taxi.

Hampton knew something was up when she saw Matthew come out of the liquor store empty handed and asked him about it.

"What did you get at the liquor store?" She gave him a suspicious look and then walked over to him and smelled his breath. "Jack, you've been drinking already! And we've got to interview a serial killer." She gave it to him with both barrels.

"I'm fine. I can handle it."

He was right. He could. Up to a point. But they had important business to deal with and Hampton didn't want anything to screw that up.

Just then, the taxi pulled up. The driver helped Hampton and Matthew into the vehicle. He smiled at them at told them that they made a nice couple. Hampton smiled when she heard those words but Matthew's face turned beet red; he was embarrassed by those words. With that, he remembered that his collar was in his jacket pocket. He retrieved it and put it on so as to not confuse anyone about his marital status. But during the ride, Hampton held Matthew's hand in hers. She remembered the night before, Matthew, however, could not. He didn't want to make waves so he allowed Hampton to keep her hand in his, until they reached the jail, then they were professional and all business.

Matthew and Hampton were met inside by Detective Firby. After shaking hands, Firby showed them to the interview room. Before entering the room, the two out-of-towners were able to see the suspect behind one-way glass. Sitting at the table in his jail house stripes, the handcuffed suspect seemed very nervous because he was fidgeting in his seat, and chewing his fingernails. He was a nearly fifty-year-old man, with a bald head on top and long, scraggly and dirty hair on the sides. His face was unshaven, wrinkled, weather-beaten, bruised, scarred and dirty. Well, at least his clothes were clean.

Firby explained to the two visitors how the suspect was caught. "Unfortunately for him, he was unexpectedly interrupted in the middle of erasing another one of his grotesquely murder victims. He was caught loading a body into his van when a patrol car drove down the alleyway and saw something suspicious going on. When they checked they actually found two bodies, not just one. Evidently, he had one already stashed there and was adding to it."

"Where was he taking the bodies?" Hampton asked.

"Don't know," Firby replied. "He wouldn't tell us. Maybe you'll have better luck."

Hampton nodded, then looked at Matthew. "Ready, Father?"

Matthew nodded and followed her into the room. They took their seats across the table from the suspect.

"A priest! What do I need a priest for?" shouted suspect Greg Pisco. "Get him outta here!" He pounded the table but then calmed down when he found out that his punches didn't hurt the table, only him.

The two remained silent. Hampton set her file on the table and opened it. She slowly looked over her notes before asking any questions, while Matthew was studying the facial expressions and body reactions of possibly his father's killer. Hampton smiled at the killer and introduced herself and Matthew.

"Mr. Pisco, I am Detective Carolyn Hampton and sitting next to me is Father Matthew. He's here today as a spectator. I'll ask the questions."

"Ask away," Pisco said in a deep, gruff voice, acting the wiseguy. "What would you like to know?"

Hampton placed a half a dozen pictures with faces on them, including Senator Strang's and John Matthew's and watched the suspect's facial expression. But there was none. He had no reaction whatsoever to the photos. "Have you seen any of those people?" Hampton asked him. "You were in our city around this time six years ago and you were there again last week. That's when Senator Strang came up missing. And we are investigating his disappearance. Can you tell us anything?"

"And what city are you talking about," asked the killer.

"The city where your cousin, Nicky Pisco lives," answered Hampton.

"Oh," he said, scratching his chin. "Yeah, I was there last week and would have returned there today had I not been caught."

"How about six years ago around this time?" Hampton asked him. "Can you remember if you were there at that time?"

He thought for a few seconds, then answered, "Yeah, I've been going there every year for more than ten years."

"Why."

"Me and my cousin work the bar every year for the Halloween Policemen's Costume Ball."

"Exactly when our victims went missing," Hampton exclaimed.

But the killer rejected her insinuation. "Hey," he barked, "I would know if I killed these people or not. And it's true, I have killed my fair share of people over the years, but the people in the photos, I've never seen them."

Hampton gave him a disgusted look, then looked over to Matthew to see what he thought about the admission. Matthew just shrugged. He would speak to her about it at a later time. Just then, Hampton decided to try a different approach. She would try threats.

"You know, Greg, we have the death penalty in our state," Hampton reminded him. "And that's what you'll get if we connect you to any of our missing victims. But if you cooperate, we can help you and probably get you twenty-five years with possibility of parole to run concurrently for any and all murders that you cop to. If not, the next time we come back will be for your extradition."

He gave her an evil look. "Is that supposed to scare me, lady?" He laughed. "I gave you my answer!"

"Let me get this straight," Hampton retorted. "The investigators believe you have left bodies in at least seventeen different states that they know of, and twenty-six different cities but you tell me you haven't left any dead bodies in my city? I don't believe it!"

He shrugged. "That's your problem," he said sarcastically.

"Why was our city so special?" Hampton asked him.

Before answering he gave Hampton a sickly smile. "Because my cousin lived there and I knew if the cops found a dead body, it might lead back to him. That's why!"

Hampton turned to Matthew and said, "Look at that, Jack, a serial killer with a conscious. Something new."

Matthew nodded.

Hampton stood up and left the room, Matthew followed.

"Is that it?" Matthew asked her, as they stood in the outer room watching the suspect.

Hampton looked at Detective Firby. "Well," she said, "we tried but didn't get very far. Maybe we'll bring more photos next time, if there is a next time."

"We'll keep you abreast of any information," Firby told the two visitors.

The three shook hands before Firby walked them to their ride to the airport. Again, they had a few hours to kill, so to get up some courage, Matthew talked Hampton into having a few drinks at the airport bar. Even with four drinks in him, she had to coax him onto the plane. Evidently, Matthew didn't trust god with his prayers. Again, Hampton held Matthew's hand throughout the flight. It frightened Matthew even more when the plane hit turbulence and rocked back and forth, up and down for more than two minutes, every second wondering if the plane was going to fall out of the sky.

But an hour and a half later, Hampton and Matthew had arrived safely at the station.

As Hampton and Matthew were saying their goodbyes, Hampton gave him a kiss on his cheek.

"Don't be a stranger," she told him before going inside. Adding, "I'll keep in touch."

Matthew told her to stop by his home anytime. "We'll have a drink or two."

The two went their separate ways. He was tired and wanted to eat something so he stopped by Gabriele's for a delicious steak and cheese hoagie. First thing he'd eaten all day, besides a bag of peanuts given to him on the airplane. He also took two to go and then left the restaurant for his abode.

While sitting in his living room listening to the news on the television, and drinking of course, he heard that a thirty-year-old school teacher from the area was missing. Another disappearance just eight days before Halloween. And this time, Matthew *knew* it wasn't the serial killer, Greg Pisco.

***

Matthew wanted to continue with his dad's investigation but then remembered he had promised to return to the mental facility to see how the elderly woman was doing. He hoped for her sake that she was at least coherent and speaking. He wanted to find her relatives and loved ones, that is, if the hospital staff hadn't done that already. He hoped it would be the last time he visited the place. It was too eerie for him from the weird trees that seemed to smother one's being as you walked beneath them to the monstrous gargoyles overlooking the property to the secluded and prison-like atmosphere; all were very depressing.

Before leaving the house, Matthew put his collar around his neck once more, to show that as a **man of god** he was a person that could be trusted.

Twenty minutes later, he was at that dreaded hospital, and sought out Nurse Brachit as soon as he entered the place. She wasn't hard to find as she found him.

"Good afternoon, Father," she said, smiling.

"Hello, Nurse Brachit. How's our patient? Any change?"

She shook her head. "No, the last time we checked she was still in a catatonic state. She hasn't responded to anything we've tried. She just sits on the floor in a cloudy daze."

He asked Brachit if he could look in on her.

"Sure. Let me get an orderly." She smelled liquor on his breath and mentioned it. "I see your wearing that same cologne, hey, Father!"

She smiled and walked away and within a minute had returned with an orderly, who led the two to the old woman's room. Brachit unlocked the door and allowed Matthew to enter with the orderly in close proximity.

Matthew kneeled down to get a closer look at the patient and lifted her face to his. Her eyes were distant, her face gaunt, a white substance drooling from her mouth. Matthew wiped the drool away with his handkerchief and asked Brachit to free her from her bonds.

"Please take her straightjacket off," he begged. "And maybe we can get a wet washrag in here so I can clean her face."

The orderly removed the straightjacket before Brachit ordered him to retrieve the washrag, pronto! He did as ordered, and returned with a wet and hot washrag, to which Matthew put to good use and washed the old woman's face and hands, all the while, the woman looking hopelessly into the Father's eyes and holding tightly onto his hands as though she didn't want him to leave her.

Just then, another nurse entered the room carrying a syringe filled with a sedative. "It's time for her sedative," the nurse told the others.

Matthew stood to leave, when suddenly the old woman spoke up, but in a nearly inaudible whisper.

"No shot! No shot," she whined to Father Matthew in a whisper as she reached out and grabbed his pant leg.

Matthew grabbed the woman's hands and kneeled down to speak with her and to hug her in his arms. "This is a joyous day for celebration," Matthew cried out, happily. "The lord has brought you back to us," he added.

"Help me," she begged him, tears falling from her eyes.

"Ma'am, what is your name?" Matthew asked her. "Do you know who you are?"

She nodded. "Yes," she whispered. "I'm Mrs. Arnold Strang."

"Are you the Senator's wife?" Brachit asked her.

The old woman nodded.

"Oh, my god," barked Matthew. "Someone call the authorities and let them know she's alive."

Matthew sat on the floor and thought back to just a few days before when he had taken her to the city's police station but they couldn't identify her and *passed the buck* over to the hospital, who *passed the buck* until she ended up in the nut house.

The nurse that had planned to give the old woman her shot quickly left the room with syringe in hand to call the authorities.

While the others in the room were waiting for the authorities to arrive, Matthew continued talking with the old woman.

"Do you remember when I found you wandering in the street and I took you to the police station?" he asked her while rubbing her hands. "Do you remember that?"

She looked into his eyes, her saddened eyes still flowing tears, and cried, "I do remember." Then suddenly, she panicked and became upset, clawing at Matthews arm. She yelled, but the words came out in a loud whisper, "I saw my husband die! They shot him while he was wearing his werewolf costume. They shot him. That costume shop is responsible. I know that costume shop is responsible. That damn costume shop." Those were the last words she spoke before passing out, most likely from exhaustion.

Soon after, the authorities came to bring her back to City hospital for observation and afterwards, hopefully, interview her about her husband's disappearance.

As they were whisking her away on a stretcher, Nurse Brachit mentioned to Matthew about another patient at the hospital who also complained about some costume shop killing his wife. "Can you believe it, Father?" she asked, shaking her head. "A costume shop that killed his wife. Does that sound rational?"

"No, it doesn't, Nurse Brachit. But I'm beginning to believe there's more to this story than meets the eye."

As the two left the room, Matthew asked her about the patient she had just described. "Can I speak to him?"

"You can speak to him... but I'm not too sure he'll speak to you."

An orderly joined them as Brachit and Matthew walked up one floor to the patient's room.

"His name is Warren Wilson," Brachit told Matthew as she unlocked the door.

The man, laying on his bed in a straightjacket, looked to be in his forties or fifties, had long, dirty hair, and long dirty toenails and was drooling from his mouth. Only a blanket and pillow was given to him for comfort besides a thin mattress.

As soon as the door opened, all you could here was the man chanting, "Costume shop. Costume shop. Costume shop." Over and over; a constant repeat of those two words that seemed to go on forever. Finally, after a few minutes of that Matthew walked over to the bed and tried to get his attention.

"Mr. Wilson. Mr. Wilson, I'm Father Matthew and I'd like to speak with you about that costume shop."

Suddenly, Mr. Wilson opened his buggy eyes and stared intently at Matthew. "Are you here to give me my last rights, Father?" he asked.

Matthew was taken aback at that question. "Why would he ask me that?" Matthew wondered. He suddenly snapped out of it and answered, "Why, are you dying?"

He said he didn't think so, but still wondered why a priest was in his room.

Matthew helped Wilson sit up so he could answer some questions. "Can I ask you some questions about this costume shop you keep chanting about? It seems you're not the only one talking about a costume shop? You didn't happen to lose your significant other at this particular costume shop, did you?"

He nodded. "My wife. Best thing that could have ever happened to me," he bragged.

"Why do you say that?" Matthew asked him.

"I always told my wife that she'd be the cause of me ending up in the nut house... and... I was right. Look at me! Where am I? In the NUT HOUSE!"

"Okay, Mr. Wilson, you don't have to yell," barked Nurse Brachit.

Matthew asked Nurse Brachit if he could have a word alone with Mr. Wilson. "I think he'll open up more if we're alone."

At first, Brachit seemed to reject the idea, but with a little more prodding from Matthew she finally relented. "You got five minutes," she snapped, adding, "And I'll be watching from the window."

She did as promised. She and the orderly left the room. Standing outside the room she watched every move of her patient through the tiny door window. Even though he was in a straightjacket, she knew he was still very delusional and dangerous. How dangerous? Last week, he put two orderlies in the hospital by head butting them each in the gut, then butting them under their chins. He knocked one guy out, who also lost a tooth in the melee and the other orderly ended up with a concussion. So Nurse Brachit wasn't taking any chances.

Matthew asked the questions and Wilson answered them, at least to the best of his ability. Whether Matthew believed him was another thing altogether. The guy wasn't speaking in four different voices simultaneously or floating in the air or vomiting a projectile four feet across the room, as Matthew had experienced during exorcisms. He was just telling his story.

Wilson explained how he and his wife were driving down I-5 highway and suddenly, out of nowhere, the car began driving itself up a steep incline and then down into a deserted valley to an almost deserted town. "The only place that had lights on was this shack with a sign over the door with the words painted on it: Costume Shop! We went inside, not knowing where we were and asked for directions back to the highway. But for some reason, we were in awe of the costumes that they had. They were really beautiful. The Costume Ball was coming up so we decided to rent costumes. My wife had tried on one, went out the door to get her purse out of the car and it was then that I experienced the worst moment of my life. She was dressed as Ma Barker and was cut down by a hundred bullets the second her foot went out the door. Then a sudden bright white light exploded and I was knocked down to the floor. The next thing I knew... was that I was locked up in this place. I remember like it was yesterday."

"What costume did you pick out?"

"Al Capone," Wilson replied. "The guy behind the counter said it was an original, and once worn by the man himself."

"Hmm," hummed Matthew. "You say you were driving down Interstate Five when all this happened?"

He nodded.

"How far from here?" Matthew believed if it was maybe two hours away then the map he found at his father's house might just show him the way.

Matthew was about to ask Wilson another question but was interrupted when Nurse Brachit came into the room.

"Time's up!" bellowed Brachit. "Mr. Wilson needs his sedative."

"Thanks, Father," Wilson said. "It was nice talking to you." He laid back on the bed and began once again chanting those two words: Costume shop! Costume shop!" Again, and again. Over and over.

But when the door finally closed, Wilson could be heard no more.

Matthew thanked Brachit and promised to **stay in touch**, although he never wanted to return to that insane asylum any time soon. The only good thing to come out of his visits so far was that Senator Strang's wife had been found alive. Even if it was in the city's nut house.

***

Matthew drove directly to the station to speak with Captain Bird about Mrs. Strang and this so-called costume shop. Arriving there, he went directly to Bird's office and asked Bird about Strang.

"She's at the hospital recuperating from her ordeal at the asylum," Bird answered.

"Thank goodness. I'm sure she feels a little better being out of that nut house, but I'm afraid she's still worried about her husband."

"Well, whatever you did, Father, seemed to work. She was lucky that you were able to bring her back to reality."

"Hey, excuse me for asking, but I know we couldn't get her name that day I brought her in, but didn't you have her photo? You were looking for her at that time, weren't you?"

Bird didn't like where Matthew was going with his insinuations. He gave him a cold stare and answered, "Hey, the Desk Sergeant made a mistake. It happens to the best of us. Anyway, it all worked out in the end."

Matthew half-heartedly agreed with him then changed the subject. "Hey, Captain, let me ask you about this costume shop. I've heard about it now from two different people. And the file you gave me mentioned a costume shop. But everything else about it was redacted."

"If it was redacted, how do you know it was about the costume shop?" Bird asked him.

"Well, I just assumed, seeing that after the word costume shop was a hyphen and after the hyphen a whole paragraph, probably ten or twelve lines was redacted."

"I haven't looked into that yet."

But Matthew wouldn't give up. He asked Bird again. "Come on! Tell me what you know. Does this costume shop have something to do with these disappearances?"

Bird sat silent. He wouldn't crack.

"Come on!" Matthew barked. "I have a right to know."

Bird wouldn't budge. If he knew anything about that costume shop, he wasn't talking.

Just then, Hampton walked into the room. Matthew turned and watched as she swayed up to the desk and handed Bird some papers. Then she was gone, like *dust in the wind*.

Matthew finally gave up trying to get an answer from Bird, at least for that day. He would try again when Bird was in a better mood. But right now, he was going to try out his map for better or worse. But first, he wanted to return home to pour himself some courage before confronting the unknown. He wanted to be ready for it.

What he wasn't ready for was Hampton's crush she had on him. Just as he was leaving, he was confronted by Hampton at the front door.

"Are you doing okay," she asked him, concerned about his drinking.

He held her hands and assured her that he was fine. "Stop by my house tonight if you like. The address is on my card I gave you. I've got something to share with you."

She told him she'd see him after dinner, around seven-thirty that evening. "I'll be done eating by then," she assured him.

He wanted to speak with her about her infatuation with him, a priest, which in his eyes and god's eyes was wrong. But Matthew knew his demons were upon him. They were testing him, his strength in god, to do what was demanded of him. The Church explicitly expressed its dissatisfaction with priests who have sexual relations with anyone. So Father Matthew was breaking his vows if he allowed his feelings to go against the Church. But then, he remembered that he was suspended from the Church, on Sabbatical. He wondered, "Was it wrong then to have an affair with a woman while away from the Church?" He thought about it and still couldn't come up with an answer. He was torn between two thoughts: one, love of woman, the other, love of god. This was Matthew's dilemma. He hoped, that through much prayer and meditation, he would come up with the correct answer.

***

After four or five double shots, Matthew was ready to travel. He would travel the two hours the map pointed out. The closest entrance to I-5 from his dad's house was just a quarter mile from Matthew's house.

Matthew would get onto the highway there, then drive for two hours at the speed limit and see what happens. It was only a two-lane highway so fifty-five miles per hour was the maximum speed allowed.

Before leaving the house, Matthew decided he may need additional courage to get him through the day so he took his bottle of whiskey with him on his ***trip to wherever.***

You did have to give it to the Father though. He had quite a big tolerance to alcohol and could handle it fairly well. It took a good fifth before another noticed his slurred words, and his wobbly walk, and that he was drunk. That's how he behaved in Rome and the reason for his suspension. He had cut back on his alcoholic content nearly in half in a short amount of time. But Matthew still had plenty of demons in his closet. He just couldn't seem to fight them as hard as the demons he exorcised, and brushed them away for the time being. Right now, he had other things on his mind. One in particular: the costume shop.

***

Matthew drove away in a happy mood. He had a good feeling he would find what he was looking for. Except, he didn't know what he was looking for. He knew it was a costume shop. But was it in a mall? Was it visible from the road? He wondered if he was going on a *wild goose chase*. He finally gave up questioning himself and was content at whatever the outcome.

He figured two hours to get there, two hours to get back and an hour investigating the costume shop, that is, if he could find it and should get back home by seven, a half hour before Hampton was to arrive. That was the plan.

The ride was fairly boring, so to pass the time he had a few swigs from his bottle of courage. In between swigs he looked at his watch.

Nearly two hours had passed and Matthew's anxiety was getting the best of him. He was on a desolate highway, no buildings, cars or people were on the horizon. He figured he had made a terrible mistake looking for a costume shop and not knowing exactly where it was. He was about to make a U-turn and drive back to the city but before he did a loud explosion occurred. A bright light exploded in front of him, blinding him for a few seconds. Before he could stop the vehicle, something or someone took control of both it and him, and suddenly the car was driving up a steep incline; going up a mountain that shouldn't be there. Matthew tried to stop the car but couldn't. He was frozen in time. Only the car was moving. Then, just as sudden as that explosion had occurred, strong winds and large hail stones began plummeting the vehicle. Balls of hail two inches in diameter began bouncing off the car, leaving large dents in its body and also cracking the windshield. Ice balls from hell is what Matthew was thinking of them but could do nothing but watch the havoc Mother Nature had brought forth. Suddenly, nearing the top of the incline, the wind lifted the vehicle into the air and transported it to the bottom of the mountain.

After catching his breath, Matthew looked around and saw only desert, tumbleweeds and cactus; nothing like this existed in his realm. He knew not where he was. However, he did see a faint light in the distance. Finally, getting his faculties under his control, he continued driving on the only road around, a dirt road, which he believed would lead him to the light and hopefully, people who could give him directions back to Interstate Five. He also wanted to learn who or what took total control of his being and why? And hoped the answers lie ahead.

Matthew followed his nose, which took him to an abandoned town. He continued past all the dilapidated and burned out, wooden shacks until he came upon the only building that seemed to be occupied, by the glowing light coming from inside. He saw a car parked near the shack and drove up to the building and parked next to it. As he got out of his car, he saw it. The thing that he had been looking for. Over the door, in big red letters were the words: *Costume Shop*! He had found it! But was it the one he was looking for? He would soon find out when he entered through the doors of the *Costume Shop*.

He was taken aback when he saw that the inside of the shop was much larger than it looked on the outside, with many thousands of different costumes scattered about. He shut the door behind him and scurried up to the front counter only to be confronted by the counter's inhabitant: a short and robust type fellow dressed up in a Joker's costume who wasn't much taller than the four feet high counter. He seemed agitated with Matthew.

"I'm sorry, sir," he said to Matthew. "But you must return your costume clean and folded. And there are no exchanges."

It took a second, but Matthew finally understood what the little man was speaking about. "Oh, no, sir," Matthew replied pointing to his clothes. "This isn't a costume, it's my profession. I'm a priest."

The Joker seemed mortified by that answer. He believed the clothes Matthew was wearing was actually one of his costumes. When he realized he was mistaken, his demeanor changed. "Oh, how can I help you?" he asked Matthew in a calm and respectful manner.

Matthew explained how he had lost his way. "I ended up here... and I don't really know how I got here. I'm kind of at a loss for words. Although, I **was** looking for a costume shop."

The Joker laughed. "Well, I guess you found it!"

Just then, a loud crash was heard. Matthew and the Joker turned and saw that a number of costumes and a manikin had fallen onto the floor. A young kid was fumbling with them, trying to return them to their proper places.

The little guy came out from behind the counter and yelled at the kid. "Hey, kid. Pick that stuff up and put it back where it belongs."

Just as the Joker was barking orders to the kid, the kid had everything back in its place. Joker let out a growl and returned to his cubicle behind the counter.

When the kid came out from behind the manikin and rows of costumes, Matthew saw that he was already in a costume, dressed as a cowboy.

"Hey, kid, who are you dressed as?" Matthew asked him.

"These are the original clothes once worn by the infamous killer who went by the name of Jim Miller, alias Deacon Jim. Isn't that right, Mr. Joker?"

Joker nodded. "Yes, they are son!"

The kid had his street clothes balled up and stuck under his arm, so he decided to put them in his car. "Mr. Joker, I'm going to put my clothes in the car." He held up his street clothes to show all concerned before going out the door.

Just as he opened the front door and took a step towards the porch, a flash of bright white light went off outside blinding everyone for a split second. Then, as the kid stepped onto the porch, a mob of vigilantes appeared out of nowhere, dragged him to the livery stable and hung him. When the stool was kicked out from beneath him, his neck snapped.

At that moment, another flash of bright white light exploded, the door shut and knocked Matthew to the floor, his head hitting the bottom molding of the counter. The blow must have knocked him out for a few minutes because when he awoke, he noticed the fall had broken his watch, the hands showing the exact time it stopped, and when he looked at the clock behind the counter it showed nearly three minutes had passed. He rushed to open the front door to see if he had been dreaming. He prayed the kid was out there. Alive! But when he opened the door… nothing! He saw only a desolate, dusty ghost town.

Matthew didn't know what to think and looked to the Joker for answers. "What the hell happened?" Matthew asked him in disbelief.

"You passed out," Joker said matter-of-factly.

"No! I mean, what happened to the kid?"

Joker played dumb. "What kid? Who are you talking about? Are you okay, Father?"

"Don't play dumb with me, you, you Joker. I know you saw him. You talked to him for crying out loud!"

Matthew stood over the little guy and came face to face with him. "You tell me now!" Matthew bellowed. "What the hell is going on here?"

Joker could smell Matthew's breath. "Have you been drinking?" Joker asked Matthew.

Matthew ignored the question, and remembered the kid's car. He had parked next to it. "The car!" he said to nobody in particular.

He stepped outside to prove the kid had been there by the kid's car. It was simple. If the car was outside the shop then the kid was inside the shop. But when he checked for it, it had disappeared. He ran around the shop, looked in front, back, to the east and west, but nothing. Then, out of the corner of his eye, he noticed movement from across the way, near what seemed to be a dilapidated blacksmith's shop. He thought he had seen a young Indian boy. Matthew looked closer but decided he had been seeing things and went back inside the costume shop.

"This place is crazy," Matthew muttered to himself as he entered the building.

"Are you okay, Father? You don't look good," Joker told him.

Matthew nodded. "I guess I have felt better at that."

"You want to sit down, Father?"

Matthew shook his head. "No, I have to get back to the city. How do I get out of here?"

"One way in, one way out," Joker replied. "Go back the way you came."

Matthew told Joker that he'd be back... maybe! "Once I figure out how I got here in the first place."

Matthew left the premises still wondering just what he had witnessed. Would he tell anyone about his outing? Would anyone believe him without any evidence? He jumped behind the wheel of his car and took the advice Joker had offered. Matthew was going back the way he came, but wondered if he'd go through that vortex again or whatever it was that took control of his car and being. He wasn't looking forward to it, so he took a few slugs from his bottle of courage. A few *big* slugs. By the time he had reached the base of the mountain, the bottle was empty. Matthew was feeling no pain. He was now ready for what was to come, whatever it may be.

A few minutes later, the car was climbing the steep incline. Towards the top, the wind began to blow, shaking the car to and fro, and a heavy rain poured down so fast that there was zero visibility. The windshield wipers couldn't move fast enough to keep up with the rain. Luckily, the car again had a mind of its own, and something had control of Matthew's mind again too. He could do nothing but sit frozen in place, that is, until the power finally released him, when it pushed him out of its realm and back into Matthew's reality and onto Interstate Five. It happened so quickly that he just missed hitting a car as his car was thrown onto the highway. He finally got the car under his control once again. At least the entity pointed it in the right direction towards the city. He looked at the dashboard clock and noticed that he had a little more than two hours before Hampton was expected to visit.

Over the next two hours Matthew wondered if he had lost his sanity. He knew he was drunk but not too drunk not to know the difference between fact and fiction. He decided to tell Hampton about his episode with the ***costume shop***.

Matthew made it home without any repercussions or mishaps, just one near miss. He pulled up into the driveway just as Hampton was walking up the steps to his porch. She turned towards the sound of the car and saw him, then met him as he got out of his car.

As they walked towards the front door, Matthew, completely out of breath, looked at Hampton in a confused manner and said, "Boy have I got something to tell you."

Leaning against him and holding his hand, she smelled the alcohol on his breath. "Whew, Jack, you've been drinking! Aren't you ever sober?"

"When I tell you what happened to me, you'll know why I need a few more drinks."

Matthew was true to his word. As soon as they walked into the house, Hampton went into the living room to sit and relax while Matthew grabbed a fresh bottle of whiskey from the kitchen cupboard and two glasses. He poured a double shot for each of them, toasted each other and then finished their drinks before a word was said.

CHAPTER 4

Matthew and Hampton had a few more drinks before Matthew spilled the beans. By the fourth drink, Hampton came and sat beside Matthew, snuggling close, her head laying on his shoulder.

"What is it you wanted to tell me?" she asked him.

He remained silent for a long thirty seconds before answering. "Carolyn, what I'm about to tell you, it doesn't go any farther than this room. Is that understood?"

"Yes, I understand."

"I don't know if what happened to me today has anything to do with the Legend of Hollow Pass but a mighty strange thing happened to me today."

Hampton placed her hand on Matthew's thigh while Matthew poured them each another drink. He handed her a glass then he sat back and began to tell his story.

"Everything happened after I went to the insane asylum and spoke to a couple of patients, but one in particular. A guy named Wilson. But that isn't important. What is important is that he was obsessed about a costume shop that made his wife disappear."

Hampton sat up and questioned him about his story. "I don't think the Legend has anything to do with a costume shop. I could be wrong but I don't think I am."

"Well Legend or not, something mighty strange happened to me today."

"Baby, are you sure you weren't having hallucinations?"

"Carolyn, I'm a Doctor of Psychology. I don't have hallucinations."

"Yeah, but you have been hitting the sauce pretty hard lately."

"You want to hear my story or not," Matthew said, spilling part of his drink on his pant leg.

Hampton patted his pant leg with some tissues but it didn't soak up the liquid so Matthew excused himself and went into the bedroom to change into a pair of dry pants.

While taking off his wet pants, Hampton came into the room and attacked him sexually. They both fell onto the bed. She crawled on top of him and began kissing him passionately. At first, he relinquished to her desires, but after realizing what was at stake he pushed her away and sat up, then quickly put on dry pants.

"I'm sorry, Carolyn, I can't go against the Church. I told you before, I took my vows. If I weren't a priest, I'd love to be in a relationship with you."

"I'm sorry too," she said, apologetically. "I didn't mean to throw myself at you."

He grabbed her hands and helped her off the bed. They walked hand in hand into the living room where Matthew continued telling his story.

"I'm driving along, following a map I found at my dad's place and after two hours of driving, I hear a loud bang, like an explosion; a flash of bright light and then, WHAM! My car is suddenly climbing up a mountain that shouldn't be there. And I have no control of it. I can't move!"

Matthew's body began to shake and perspiration began to flow from his pores. Hampton saw what was happening and poured him a double shot from the whiskey bottle. She handed him the glass but saw that he was too weak to hold it so she put the glass to his mouth and tipped it so it would flow easily into his mouth. She did this until he had finished the drink. That seemed to settle his nerves and shakes.

"Now, just take your time, honey. Finish your story."

Matthew cleared his throat and continued telling his story. "So, my car started climbing up a mountain that shouldn't have been there and I couldn't do a thing about it. I was frozen to my seat. I couldn't move. I could barely think. Then it started hailing. Hail as large as baseballs started raining down, pummeling my car."

"I wondered how you got all those dents in your car," said Hampton interrupting Matthew's story telling.

Matthew seemed frustrated for her interruption. Hampton noticed and told him to continue.

"I'm sorry, honey."

"So, something has control of both me and the car, then suddenly a gust of wind picks up the car and I end up on the other side of the mountain and in a valley. And just as the car lands on the ground I get back control of my faculties. So, I look around and the only thing I see besides desert is a light off in the distance. So, I drive towards the light and I find what I think I've been looking for: that costume shop. It's the only building that showed any signs of life. Everything around it was abandoned and dilapidated. It looked like a ghost town that had been abandoned centuries ago. Then I noticed another car parked near the shack of the costume shop so I parked next to it and went into the shop, and standing behind the counter was a midget dressed up as a Joker. And he wasn't just dressed up as one, but that was his actual name: Joker."

"Honey, this story is getting weirder and weirder," interjected Hampton as she poured the two another drink.

Matthew chugged his drink, then continued. "While I was asking the little guy behind the counter a question, I heard a commotion to my right and saw that a guy, probably in his early twenties, was wearing a costume of some killer cowboy. When he opened the door to go outside..."

He stopped speaking. Hampton filled his glass once again with his instant courage. He chugged that one down too and finished the story. "When he stepped outside, I saw or think I saw a mob grab him and hang him from a livery stable. I mean, this happened in a split second. Then there was a bright flash of light, and an invisible force knocked me to the floor. I passed out for a good two or three minutes. When I woke up, the door was closed. When I checked outside, there was nothing. Not even the kid's car that I parked next to. Then I rode back the way I came, had a similar experience leaving as I had going, and finally made it home. What a crazy experience! Not even my exorcisms were as crazy. Geez!"

Hampton agreed with him. "You're right. You had a crazy experience. I think your drinking caught up with you."

"Christ, Carolyn, I'm not crazy… *or drunk*! I can hold my liquor. And I have a PHD in Psychology. Don't you think I know I don't sound rational?"

"Take it easy, honey," Carol whispered into his ear. "Why don't we get you ready for bed?"

Matthew chugged one last shot before retreating to his bedroom with Hampton in tow. They both fell onto the bed together with Hampton laying on top of him. She gave him a playful kiss on the lips, then helped him get out of his clothes and into bed before undressing herself and laying right next to him, both completely naked. She knew that she was too drunk to drive home and decided to stay with her new love, Father Jack Matthew, whom she had only known for a few days but in her mind, they clicked immediately. She was in love with him. But was he in love with her or the Church? She didn't care. She was now in charge and took advantage of Matthew's intoxication.

Matthew awoke early the next morning and found himself naked. Hampton was lying next to him, also naked.

To say the least, he was flabbergasted at the thought of being a sexual toy for her. He wondered if she had performed intercourse on him during the night. He would ask her in due time. But first he needed to shower and dress before asking Hampton the important question. He was at a loss for words. One part of him was embarrassed by the fact that he may have been raped by a beautiful woman, but then, the other half of him was downright giddy over the fact that this beautiful woman wanted him. But he wasn't sure if anything had happened. He would ask her that question when the time was right.

Matthew, to say the least, was confused. His mind was still cloudy from the night before. He remembered parts of the conversation they had but not much else. He hoped Hampton would refresh his memory.

It wasn't that long before Matthew got his answer.

By the time Hampton washed and dressed, Matthew had already started the morning off with cereal, chased with two double shots of whiskey. That gave him the burst of energy needed to put his plan together. A plan that included Hampton.

She came into the kitchen and sat at the table. Matthew poured her a cup of coffee and finally asked her that important question.

"What happened last night? I woke up naked... with you laying naked next to me. Carol, I am a man of god and forbade to lay with anyone."

She chuckled. "Don't worry, baby. Nothing happened, other than we went to sleep in the nude. I promise." She leaned over and gave him a peck on the cheek.

He scolded her for putting him in that position. "It could be misconstrued," he told her.

"Oh, you know you like it," she teased.

"Please, Carolyn, I'm a Father of the Cloth. If I weren't with the Church, it might be a different story. But I am. So please, from now on we must conduct ourselves as professionals if we want to continue to work together."

She apologized for being so forward and promised to conduct herself in a professional manner, then added, "But I still think you're cute."

"Well I think you're cute too," Matthew replied, throwing back another shot. "Now that we have that settled, I need your help with a plan I've come up with."

"What plan is that?" She was curious.

"I want us to visit this place that I visited yesterday. I want to prove to you that I wasn't seeing things, that I wasn't delusional. I want to gather evidence and prove that this place exists. I'm leaning towards the belief that this costume shop might have something to do with that Legend everyone's talking about."

"You've got to be kidding!"

"No! I'm not kidding. I think the costume shop is where those spirits are taking the souls that they believe is owed to them. It's just a theory for now. But maybe I can find a way to prove my theory. Do you have a cell phone with a camera?"

"Yes, of course. Why?"

He told her that he wanted her to record their visit.

She had an idea. "Listen, I don't want them to know I'm recording. Someone there might ask questions if they see me doing that. I've got a camera purse on my desk at the station. If we stop there first I can grab it. That way, no one will ever know that I'm recording our undercover work."

Matthew was anxious to get going. "Great!" he exclaimed. "Let's get going. It'll take us two hours to get there."

Hampton finished her coffee and off they went, Matthew driving, of course. The first stop, the station, to retrieve her camera purse and to sign in. While she was there she told Captain Bird her plans for the day.

"I'm working with Father Matthew. We're following a lead."

He wished her good luck as she walked out of his office.

A minute later, she was back in Matthew's car, heading for god-only-knows. She had absolutely no idea where they were headed. That was in Matthew's hands. She was just along for the ride.

"Hey," Matthew said, breaking the silence. "When I tell you, I want you to turn on the camera and set it on the dashboard so we can record the second the mountain appears. I'm telling you, Carolyn, it appears instantaneously. A second before the phenomenon happens… there's only flat land for miles… but, wham! There it is!"

Matthew pulled out a bottle of whiskey from under his seat and had Hampton grab two cups from the backseat. He then had her pour each of them a stiff drink. Against her better judgement, she did as ordered. She knew he could hold his liquor… to a point.

***

As the two-hour mark came upon them, Matthew had Hampton start the camera. She did, then set the purse on the dashboard and waited. But nothing out of the ordinary happened. Another twenty minutes of driving and still, no mountain! Matthew couldn't understand it.

Hampton tried to console him. "Come on, honey," she said soothingly. "Don't be too hard on yourself. Maybe it was just your imagination playing tricks on you."

"Please, Carol," snapped Matthew, "don't patronize me. I'm not a child."

Matthew wasn't really angry, but more frustrated than anything. He was embarrassed that everything he had expected to show her never materialized. He wondered, why? "There has to be a reason for it," he thought to himself.

They drove back to the city in silence. Matthew was in deep thought for the two-hour return trip. As they reached his home Matthew had an idea.

"Hey, I think I may have the answer," he exclaimed.

But Hampton was confused. "Answer? Answer to what?"

"Answer to what? This mystery. Of why the mountain didn't appear that leads to that costume shop."

Matthew was frustrated and angry. Hampton could see that. So, she tried to change the subject. But Matthew only had one thing on his mind. And that was: the costume shop. He was going to get back there if he had to use the wrath of god to do it. There was a good reason that the phenomenon didn't appear and he was going to find out. Then it hit him.

"Hey," Matthew said, thinking out loud, "if that costume shop is part of the Legend and the Legend claims that the Indian spirits are taking descendants of the people who massacred that Indian tribe, then I'd bet you aren't a descendant. And that's the reason why nothing happened today. I want to get on the Internet and see if I can get a list of names of people that were involved in that massacre and their descendants that are, say living within a fifty-mile radius."

"I thought you didn't believe in the Legend of Hollow Pass," replied Hampton.

"Well, I don't... Yet!" Matthew took one last swig from his bottle and placed it back under his seat.

A few minutes later, the two were relaxing in Matthew's living room, having a drink and surfing the Web for answers.

Matthew found the site he needed. It listed both the names of Hollow Pass townspeople during the year of the massacre and also gave a list of the names of over fifty descendants. As Matthew printed out the lists of names, Hampton was checking out the names on the monitor and noticed one that looked familiar.

"Hey, here's a name that I know. In fact, she's a detective in my department."

"What's her name?" Matthew asked.

She pointed to the name on the monitor.

Matthew read aloud the name: "Janet Wellman. You say she's a detective?" he asked Hampton.

Hampton nodded. "Yes. She's been in the department nearly as long as I have. We went to the Academy together."

Matthew sat thinking, thinking his next move. Then a light bulb went off in his head. He looked to Hampton for an answer. "I wonder if Captain Bird would let Wellman work with me on my investigation. I want her to take the same ride we took today, and see what happens. If we don't succeed, I won't try again and I'll blame my delusions on my drinking."

"You don't want to work with her," snapped Hampton. "She's the department slut!"

"Hey, Hey!" barked Matthew. "What brought that on?"

She apologized to Matthew for showing her jealousy.

"I just don't like her," she retorted.

But Matthew gave her a good reason for wanting Wellman's help. "If she can help us find out where our missing people are, then so be it. I'd take the help from the devil himself if we could find out what happened to those people who disappeared."

Matthew pulled no punches. He told it like it is. He wasn't going down without a fight. He was going to prove whether he was delusional or rational. If Wellman could help him do that, then that's what needed to be done.

***

Matthew and Hampton left for the station immediately. Time was dissipating fast. There weren't many days left until Halloween and then, the disappearances would stop. So Matthew would have to act fast to make any headway into the Legend of Hollow Pass.

While Matthew was in Bird's office speaking to Bird about Wellman, Hampton was at Wellman's desk speaking with her concerning Matthew and his problem.

After listening to Matthew, Bird called Wellman into his office.

Bird spoke to Wellman directly. "After speaking with Father Matthew" he told her, "concerning his investigation into his father's disappearance he has requested your help in tracking down a lead."

"I thought Hampton was helping him," she whined.

Bird told her differently. "Hampton's busy following leads on her case."

"Whatever," Wellman retorted. She looked at Matthew. "Do you need me today?"

Matthew nodded. "I need you to follow me." Adding, "We need to take a ride."

Wellman followed Matthew as they left Bird's office. As Matthew was leaving, Hampton met him at the front door and whispered "sweet nothings" into his ear.

Matthew shot back. "I'm a priest, Carolyn. Stop that!"

Everyone in the room looked shocked over the words that came out of Father Matthew's mouth and wondered what words Hampton had whispered into his ear to make Matthew frustrated and angry.

***

While riding in the car, Matthew asked Wellman some questions about her faith and her opinion on the Legend of Hollow Pass.

"Are you a person of faith, Detective?" he asked her.

"Janet. Call me Janet, Father."

"You don't have to call me Father. You can call me Jack."

"Okay, Jack. Yes, I am a person of faith. I belong to the Baptist Church. Why?"

"I have a question to ask you and I want your honest opinion. No matter how crazy the question sounds. Okay?"

She agreed. "I just hope it's not about you and Hampton."

"What," Matthew barked. "What about me and Hampton?"

She told him that Hampton had a crush on him. "She's told others that she was having an affair with you."

"I don't believe it. I'm a priest for Christ sake! I'll have to speak with her about that."

"Yeah, some women have an infatuation with priests," she told him. "I guess you're in that category."

"Did she mention anything about my drinking?"

"She did say that you were a heavy drinker."

"Do you drink?" he asked her.

"Are you kidding? In my profession… it's a necessity. Especially, this time of year."

"What's so special about this time of year? You're not talking about the Legend of Hollow Pass, are you?"

"Well, I'm talking about the number of disappearances that happen during the two weeks before and up to Halloween. Whether the Legend of Hollow Pass has anything to do with those disappearances or not, is still up in the air. Right now, we're looking at that serial killer they're holding in Chicago for a number of disappearances. But the Legend is exactly what it is: a legend… that's grown over the decades."

"So, you don't think the Legend of Hollow Pass exists?"

She shook her head, then explained her position on the subject. "As far as history goes, yes there was a town called Hollow Pass that was built near a tribe of Indians. And yes, those townspeople massacred the entire village, men women and children. But that's as far as it goes."

"What about the curse?"

"Yes, I believe those Indians before they died, cursed the killers, and yes, it was written that all or most of those townspeople that committed that massacre died from the plague. But do I believe that those Indian spirits are taking present day souls, the descendants of the killers? I don't think so." She stated her opinion with authority.

Matthew wanted to tell her the real reason she was with him, but first needed a little courage. He pulled his half full bottle of whiskey from under the seat and before Wellman could object, Matthew took a long swig from the bottle. He then passed it to Wellman. "Take a swig," Matthew told her. "You'll need it if this works out like I think it will."

She looked at him confused by his motives. "Why do I need to drink? What's going to happen?"

"Take a healthy swig and I'll tell you. You need to be relaxed and this stuff will relax you." He pressed the bottle into her hand.

"Oh, what the hell!" She grabbed the bottle and took a healthy swig, then handed it back to Matthew.

He took the bottle out of her hand and took another swig before readying himself and her for the phenomenon.

"We have about five minutes," Matthew told her, "before something strange will happen. Did you bring the camera purse?"

"Camera purse? I don't have a camera purse. You didn't tell me to bring one."

Matthew asked her if she had her cell phone. "I need you to record whatever happens. So, get it out and start recording. We should be near the area any minute."

She was frightened with uncertainty of what was to come.

She took her cell phone from her purse but found out that it needed to be charged. The battery was dead. Matthew was beyond himself when he learned that he wasn't able to record the entire episode. His phone was more than eight years old and had no camera. He would have to be satisfied with a live witness to the phenomenon. But first, he had to prove that the phenomenon actually existed. Just as he was doubting his sanity, a bright light exploded, and within an instant, the vehicle began climbing a steep incline and the two investigators, frozen in their seats. They tried speaking, but to no avail.

Matthew's hands were glued to the steering wheel but yet, had no control of his vehicle. Hampton's body was glued to the seat and her face frozen, as she tried to scream at that exact moment the phenomenon showed its face.

Mother Nature again pummeled the car with everything she could muster: hurricane winds and rain, a black sky with lightning bolts exploding all around them before finally coming to a halt at the bottom of the other side. As the car hit the ground with a hard thud, the shockwave knocked the two occupants back into reality.

Matthew was back in familiar territory once again. For Wellman, she was still in shock and thought she had ingested a hallucinogenic that was placed into the whiskey.

"Did you put something in that whiskey?" she asked suspiciously.

"Of course not," Matthew replied as he put the car into gear and headed for the ghost town and its costume shop.

"What the *hell's* going on? I don't believe this shit! We're driving in a desert and we have no desert."

Matthew smiled. "Janet, we are going to make history today. We will prove that the Legend of Hollow Pass actually exists."

"What's this place got to do with the Legend?"

"I'm not real sure yet, but if it doesn't have anything to do with it, then where are we… and what just happened to us? We are headed for the only building that's still standing and the rest of what once was a town, was mostly burned down to the ground, probably to get rid of the disease."

"I think I need a drink."

"I know what you mean," Matthew replied.

"No, I mean I need a drink. Give me the whiskey," she demanded.

He pulled the bottle from under the seat and handed it to her. "Hurry up. We'll be at the shop any minute."

She grabbed the bottle from him and took a long swig, so long that she had to stop to catch her breath. Matthew grabbed the bottle from her before she became too drunk to walk. He didn't know what type of tolerance she had to alcohol; and didn't want to find out today. He needed her alert and aware of her surroundings.

Matthew put the bottle back under his seat and finally pulled up to the shop and parked his car next to another.

"What do I do?" Wellman asked Matthew.

"Just follow my lead. Maybe we can finally get to the bottom of what's ever going on in this god forsaken place."

"Will do!"

Wellman followed Matthew into the shop not knowing what to expect. She still had her doubts about what was actually happening.

"I'm back," Matthew said to the little guy behind the counter.

"I didn't think I'd see you again, Father," said Joker. "Who's your friend?" As he peered over the counter and smiled at the pretty woman the bells on his costume clanged with excitement.

Matthew introduced her. "This is my good friend, Janet Wellman. She's here today hoping to find some people who disappeared and we think the last place they visited was this costume shop. Would you know anything about that, Mr. Joker?"

Before he could answer, a young couple came out from the small back room dressing room wearing their costumes.

"Don't tell me," Matthew said to the couple, "you're dressed as Bonny and Clyde. Am I right?"

"That is correct," Clyde replied. "And I see you're going to a party as a priest."

Matthew told them he wasn't wearing a costume. "Everyone thinks that when I'm in a costume shop."

Matthew asked them their names.

"I'm Toby Johnson," he replied.

"And my name is Karen Craig."

Matthew didn't mince words and got right to the point. "Did your ancestors come from this area around the time of the Civil War?"

"Yes," they said in unison.

"I figured as much or they wouldn't be here," Matthew whispered to Wellman.

"What was that?" asked Toby.

"Nothing," Matthew answered. "I was talking to myself."

Toby asked his girlfriend to take their clothes to the car.

But Matthew warned her. "Don't go out there with your costume on."

"They have to wear them out of the shop," shouted Joker.

"But if you know what's good for you, you won't," Matthew warned the two kids. "I'm begging you."

"Why, what's going to happen?" Wellman asked Matthew in a whisper.

Matthew didn't answer and remained silent.

The couple didn't listen to Matthew and his pleas.

"We have a party to go to," Toby barked, and walked right past him toward the door.

But before the door could be opened, Matthew grabbed Toby's wrist and arm to hold him back and not let him leave. Matthew, however, didn't have control of the girl. When she opened the door, Matthew jumped at her, trying to grab her arm and keep her from going outside. But as they were wrestling, Matthew tripped and pushed them towards and through the open door. The second the two kids tumbled through that open door, a blinding light exploded, and hundreds of gunshots rang out, killing them both. Within a nanosecond, it was over. The door slammed shut, but before it did, a stray bullet found its way into the shop. Matthew, unfortunately, was also a victim of those gunshots. One bullet slammed into his upper shoulder, went through his body and landed in the counter's molding.

Wellman was upset and dumbfounded after witnessing the two kid's shooting. She couldn't believe what she had seen. Even though she was in shock, she helped Matthew get to his feet. He wasn't as injured as first thought. The bullet merely went through his suit jacket, burning and blistering his skin in the process.

As Matthew limped to the front door and opened it, he knew that those two kids had disappeared along with their vehicle. He wanted Wellman to witness everything that had happened and coaxed her to him. He opened the door and watched Wellman's expression.

"Where did they go?" she asked him in disbelief.

"They disappeared into the night," Matthew replied, sarcastically.

Wellman walked up and down the street, around the shop, everywhere possible looking for the two kids. Then she noticed their car had also disappeared.

"Look," she shouted to Matthew, "their car's gone too!" She just couldn't get it through her head that this had really happened. "Maybe all this was a magic trick." She hoped, anyway.

"Yeah, a trick done by the Indian spirits," Matthew said to no one in particular.

"Boy," Wellman said seemingly exhausted from the strange experience, "I need a drink!"

"Me, too. But later. I have to speak with Joker."

The two investigators returned to the shop to speak with Joker, but he couldn't speak. It seemed there were two stray bullets that found their way into the shop. One hit Matthew, the other, Joker. He was on the floor lying dead behind the counter, but no blood; even though a bullet had passed through his forehead and exited the back of the head, then slammed into the wall behind the counter, there wasn't a drop of blood to be found.

Matthew kneeled down to check his vitals, but to no avail. The little guy was dead as dead could be.

Matthew turned and asked Wellman for a costume big enough to cover the body. She retrieved one large enough and brought it to him. He took it from her hands and turned back around to cover the body. But within those few seconds of looking away, the body was nowhere to be found. He had disappeared; completely. Only the Joker outfit lay on the floor.

Wellman again couldn't believe her eyes. "I really need a drink now!" she said to no one in particular. "This is too crazy for me. Let's get out of here, Jack."

"Yeah, I think you're right. It's time to go home."

They really didn't have any other choice. The shop was empty. But before leaving, Matthew noticed a folded-up piece of paper lying on the floor near the door and picked it up. He hadn't noticed it before. He unfolded it and looked to see what it was and then saw there was writing on it. The author wrote, in big black letters that looked to be written in charcoal: HELP US! That's all it said. Matthew wondered if someone had dropped it or if someone, during that split second, had thrown it into the shop. He placed the paper into his jacket pocket and got out of there. The two investigators were in disbelief and shock and couldn't get into the car fast enough. Matthew was still feeling a little pain from the shoulder burn and Wellman was feeling a little lost and very inadequate.

As soon as they started back the way they came, Matthew grabbed the bottle of whiskey from under the seat and handed it to Wellman. She couldn't get the bottle to her lips fast enough and drank two big swigs, which left just about the same for Matthew.

"Damn, I needed that," she boasted. "What the hell are we going to tell Captain Bird about this?" She handed the bottle to Matthew and he finished it in one gulp.

"I needed that too. I think much worse than you," he told her. "And as far as Bird goes, I don't know what to tell him. We have to think about that. I wish we had another bottle."

"I'd second the motion," she answered.

"Are you hungry?" he asked her.

She nodded.

"Do you like Hoagies?"

"Yeah, they're okay."

"Good! We'll pick some up at Gabriele's Hoagies."

"I don't think I'm in any shape to go inside."

"Then, we'll get them at the 'Drive Thru' and go back to my place and eat them, then maybe have a few drinks and figure out what we're going to tell Bird."

"That sounds good to me. I need to relax and get my head on straight. If I told anyone about what I've seen today, they'd send *me* to the insane asylum."

Matthew let out a sickly laugh. "That's why we need evidence. If we had had a camera with us today and filmed everything that we saw, we'd be on every television news show in the country. Heck, the Church would probably promote me to Bishop." He laughed.

"I see now why Hampton has a crush on you, Jack. You are…"

She didn't get to finish her sentence. They had reached the base of Hollow Pass Mountain and that invisible force had taken control of the car and their beings once again.

Mother Nature's wrath boomed once again. The two occupants were at her mercy and that of the spirits. However, they made it through without any repercussions. As the vehicle came through it all with just a few more bumps and bruises, the mountain disappeared as quickly as it had appeared and the area returned to the way it had been: Flat farming land as far as the eye could see.

But as the vehicle was thrown out of the spirit world and back into the real world, it almost came crashing into a vehicle that was traveling on the same road. Luckily, Matthew was able to, in a split second, turn the car away from ramming into the other car and came to a screeching halt. Thank god, nobody was hurt.

After a few seconds to catch their breath, Matthew took control of his car and continued on his way towards home, stopping first at Gabriele's to pick up three or four hoagies.

Soon after, the two were sitting in Matthew's living room drinking heavily trying to figure out what they had seen. While drinking and talking, Wellman dressed Matthew's wound and to do that, Matthew had to disrobe his jacket and shirt. She liked what she saw. Matthew was in good shape and she noticed.

"Now I know why Hampton has a crush on you," she said, as she rubbed Matthew's shoulder. "You are a woman's dream.

They continued drinking, and the more they drank their talking became more intimate. Wellman began flirting with Matthew, snuggling close against his naked chest, rubbing his hair, giving him light kisses on the cheek but Matthew was having none of it and tried to move away, but as exhausted as he was he didn't have the strength.

They both just curled up on the couch and took a short nap, which was interrupted by an angry Carolyn Hampton. When she knocked on the door there was no answer, so she let herself in through the unlocked door. She called out but still no answer. Seconds later, in the living room, Hampton discovered a half-naked Matthew with Wellman by his side. Seeing that made Hampton very upset and angry.

"You dirty slut," Hampton shouted to a waking Wellman. "I knew this was going to happen!"

Hampton stood over Wellman and spewed foul language, calling Wellman every foul name in the book. Matthew tried to calm the situation by telling Hampton that nothing had happened.

"She was just dressing my wound," Matthew told her, pointing to his shoulder and bandages.

Hampton wasn't buying it. "Bull," snarled Hampton. "You were sleeping together."

"Carolyn," Matthew begged. "You must leave before something bad happens. Your jealousy is just too crazy. I told you before, I'm a man of the cloth. I have chosen god over love. I'm sorry, that's just the way it is. We'll talk about this another time. But coming in here unannounced and acting as though we are a couple is purely asinine. So please, get out of my house until you calm down."

"But…" Hampton tried to speak but Matthew refused to listen and pointed towards the door. She finally got the hint, and slowly walked away and out of the house.

Just before leaving, she shouted, "I'll call you later, Jack."

The two remaining decided to sober up and talk about their next steps into their investigation of the Legend of Hollow Pass and the nexus it had with their missing person's investigations.

Matthew put on a clean suit of clothes and then went into the kitchen and had coffee with Wellman. They talked about their upcoming meeting with Captain Bird.

"What are we going to tell him?" Wellman asked Matthew.

Matthew took a sip of his coffee, then said, "Nothing! Not until we get some evidence. And I plan to get it."

Wellman was hesitant. She really didn't want to return to that place. "Do you really need my help?" she asked him.

He nodded. "You have the camera phone. I want you to get it. We'll go back tomorrow."

She tried to talk him out of it. "We can show Captain Bird that piece of paper you found on that floor. That's evidence." She looked very apprehensive.

Matthew told her that he wanted to *stall* Bird for extra time. "We need at least one more day before we reveal anything to Bird. If this works out, we'll be revealing our story to the world... that the Legend of Hollow Pass actually exists, and when we do, we'll either be labeled as lunatics or saviors. So be prepared."

Wellman took a deep breath, one last sip of coffee and off they went, out the door and straight to the station.

CHAPTER 5

Matthew and Wellman were standing in front of Captain Bird fifteen minutes after leaving the house.

Sitting in the room was Amy Strang, hoping for an update on the whereabouts of her father.

"Boy, you two looks like hell!" Bird told Matthew and Wellman.

"We're sorry, Captain," said Wellman apologetically. "We were chasing down some leads."

As Wellman was speaking, Hampton was roaming the hall, pacing in front of Bird's door trying to hear what was being said.

Bird noticed but then paid no attention as his attention turned back to Matthew and Wellman. "So what do you got for me?" he asked them.

"Nothing yet," Matthew replied. "But we're on a hot lead."

Bird looked to Wellman for an answer. "What about it, Wellman?"

She stalled for a good minute.

"Well," Bird asked her, feeling she wasn't telling him all she knew.

Wellman looked to Matthew. "Give me that paper."

He shook his head and refused her request.

Again, Wellman ordered Matthew to surrender the paper.

He again refused. "I can't in good conscious give it to you."

Wellman hit him lightly on the arm and demanded the paper.

Finally, Matthew reluctantly reached into his jacket pocket and pulled out a folded piece of paper and handed it to her.

She, in turn, unfolded the paper and handed it to Bird. "Here you go, sir," she said, as she handed the paper to him.

Strang leaned forward in her seat to get a better look at the evidence being handed to the Captain.

Bird read it, then said, "Help us! Help who?"

Wellman gave him a quizzical look. "We can't tell you that yet, sir," Wellman answered. "We need at least one more day for further investigation."

Just then, Strang stood up and snatched the paper from Bird's hand. She read the words out loud. "Help us!" She looked at the words again, longer this time. She then realized that the writing was in her daddy's handwriting. "This looks like my daddy's handwriting," she told them. She turned to Matthew and Wellman. "Where did you find this?"

Strang was becoming hysterical and very upset. She wanted answers. But Matthew and Wellman had none to give her… yet. They couldn't say a word about what they had witnessed. Without evidence, they would be the laughing stock of the department. Even though Matthew wasn't really a verified police detective, although he had the credentials to be one, he would still be looked down upon among the City's finest and be considered a piranha. The trust between him and the department would be shattered and lost forever if he told such an outrageous story without the evidence to back it up.

So, Matthew and Wellman promised Bird and Strang that an update on the disappearance of Senator Strang and others would be forthcoming within a day or so.

"Please be patient," Matthew told Strang. To change the subject, he asked about her mother. "How's she doing?"

"She's fine. Thank you."

"I wish we could stay longer, but we have work to do," interjected Wellman.

Matthew and Wellman moved towards the open door and were met there by Hampton. She seemed upset about something. The three of them huddled just outside the door. Then suddenly, Hampton exploded.

"You filthy whore!" Hampton screamed and pulled Wellman's hair.

"Stop that," Wellman yelled, grabbing and pinching Hampton's hands to get them out of her hair.

Before anyone in the department could act and pull the two pussy cats away from each other, Bird heard and saw the commotion and came out to break it up.

"What's wrong with you two," Bird said, in a scolding manner. "You are detectives and professionals, act like it."

Before leaving, Bird had one other thing to say to Matthew and company. "You two ladies are too involved with Father Matthew. I think it's best that you stay away from him until further notice."

Matthew pleaded with Bird to change his mind. "Please, Captain. I really need the expertise of Detective Wellman."

Bird wouldn't budge. He gave Matthew an ultimatum. "I'll have Wellman's replacement for you by tomorrow. Be satisfied with that or you can work on your investigation alone."

Reluctantly, Matthew relinquished and half-heartedly agreed with a replacement. "Male or female?" he asked, sarcastically.

Bird snickered and went back into his office.

As Hampton returned to her desk fuming, Matthew and Wellman walked together to the front door. Before leaving Matthew told Wellman he still needed her help. "Call in sick tomorrow."

She asked him, why?

"I need you to get the camera purse and meet me at my house in the morning at seven," he whispered to her.

She nodded. "See you then."

Wellman returned to her desk and had to put up with Hampton staring at her with evil eyes till the end of the shift. Hampton looked as though she wanted to tear Wellman apart for getting too close to *her* man.

***

Matthew returned home and started exercising his arm immediately. Thank goodness there were no women around to interfere with his drinking. He sat on the couch in his living room, drinking and thinking, thinking about what tomorrow would bring and how he would bring his revelations about the Legend not only to Captain Bird but to the whole world. He would show his recording of Hollow Pass and the Costume Shop to the nonbelievers and naysayers. Once they viewed it, he was certain nobody could deny the presence of a spirit world. This would bring notoriety to not only Matthew but to the Church. He wasn't too sure if that was a good or bad thing, but was sure to find out…and very soon.

He was sure the people viewing the recording would be surprised by the evidence.

Not only would the people be surprised, but Matthew was surprised by a loud pounding on the front door. After drinking nearly half a fifth of whiskey, he was slow to move. More pounding occurred.

"Okay, okay, I'm coming," he shouted, as he lifted himself off the couch and walked slowly to his front door.

As he opened it he was surprised to see Detective Hampton standing on the porch.

"Hello, honey," she purred with a smile, and then walked into Matthew's abode uninvited.

Matthew tried to keep her in the foyer but she walked past him and into the living room. Matthew followed. She sat down on the couch and made her presence known.

"Can I have a drink, Jack?" She pointed to the half empty bottle sitting on the end table.

He nodded and poured her a drink then sat next to her. "After this, though, Carolyn, you'll have to go. I have to get up early tomorrow morning."

"What's so important about tomorrow," she said, as she leaned up against him and rubbed her body on his like a cat to its owner.

Matthew didn't know what to tell her, then decided on the truth. "Wellman and I are chasing some leads."

"I thought Captain Bird forbid her to work with you and he was going to get you another detective to help you."

"She's calling in sick tomorrow. She'll be helping me on her own time."

"She's a slut!" Hampton snarled.

"Carolyn, what is your problem? Why all this hostility against Wellman? She's helping me do the job you couldn't do."

"And what's that?"

"Wellman is helping me get the evidence to prove that the Legend of Hollow Pass actually exists."

"Are you serious?" she asked as she poured herself another drink.

"Yes, you know we're both descendants of killers from long ago. We have found a way into the spirit world. And the people that are taken are taken to a far different spirit world. Hollow Pass is a spirit world within a spirit world."

Hampton was dumbfounded by the words spoken by Matthew. When they first met, Hampton explained the Legend to Matthew to the best of her ability from stories she had heard while investigating missing person cases. Even after everything Matthew was told, he still didn't believe in the Legend.

"I remember asking you," said Hampton, "or you asking me... about the Legend of Hollow Pass and after telling you the history behind the Legend, you told me that you didn't believe in it. But now, you're adamant about this 'spirit world within a spirit world'. You sound ridiculous.

If you told any sane person that story, they would say your nuts. I mean believing in god is one thing, but the Legend! Come on, Jack."

"That's why we're going to bring back the evidence to prove or disprove that the Legend of Hollow Pass exists."

"Well, I still wish you wouldn't work with her and wait for your replacement. I don't like that broad. There's just something about her."

"I'm sorry, Carolyn, but it's getting late and you'll have to leave. I have to get up early in the morning and before I go to bed I have to eat something."

Matthew helped Hampton stand up and then walked her to her car.

"Goodnight, Carolyn. Drive Careful."

Hampton gave him a peck on the cheek. "I'll see you tomorrow," she told him as she got into her car and drove away.

Matthew couldn't get rid of her fast enough. He would prove to her and all that there actually was a spirit realm invisible to all but a few souls that were tricked and taken to their final destination. He hoped to change the rules. Knowing his background in psychology and exorcism, once the evidence was known and proven that the place actually existed, the Church couldn't deny Matthew's reinstatement in the Church. Then, hopefully, he could get permission from the Vatican and fight these spirits and demons and return the people that were taken back to the realm from which they came.

Matthew had had a rough day and was worn out. He drank one last shot of whiskey while he ate a cold steak and cheese hoagie before turning in for the night.

He fell asleep, as all other nights in a drunken haze. Usually, he couldn't remember his dreams, but on this particular night he awakened twice, to the same nightmare, over a period of five hours from the first time he awakened to the second. Each time he woke up in a sopping sweat, so wet that he had to change t-shirts and boxers. In his dream, Matthew saw a little deformed man standing behind the counter at the costume shop that kept telling him to: "Jump thru door." Over and over.

As the little deformed man spoke, raging fireballs shot from his mouth, hitting Matthew in the chest. Fast action on Matthew's part, was able to put the flames out of a few but the fireballs began exploding on him in machine gun-like bursts. Matthew tried to flee through the open door, but the fire took control of him and finally consumed his body entirely until black ash formed and fell to the ground. The strong winds coming through the open door spread the ash among the costumes and shop. As soon as the ash had disappeared Matthew would wake up. After this happened a second time, Matthew decided to stay awake and drink lots of coffee, that is, as long as it also had lots of whiskey mixed in. He had nearly two hours to kill before Wellman was due. So, he made himself some toast and scrambled eggs before showering and dressing. He would again wear his collar but this time also bring Holy water, just in case he found a way to battle those demons.

While shaving he noticed that he had a few more wrinkles on his forehead and his hair had turned a light gray overnight. However, he wasn't too concerned. In fact, that thought had completely left his mind as soon as he left the bathroom. He went into the kitchen to have more coffee and turned on the small television sitting on the counter. A news reporter came on and mentioned that two more citizens from the area were missing.

Matthew choked on his coffee when he heard the names of the missing people: a twenty-four year old male named Toby Johnson and a twenty-three year old female named Karen Craig. These missing people were the two he had met at the Costume Shop. He was in a quandary. He wanted to tell anyone that would listen about those two kids and their demise, but didn't want to take the chance without having hard evidence. Matthew couldn't tell anyone about seeing them disappear right before his eyes just after they were pummeled with machine gun fire, which cut them in two. No one would believe him until he had ***hard evidence*** that could be seen and heard. He hoped and prayed that day would be today.

Matthew had drunk nearly a pint of coffee mixed with a heavy dose of whiskey by the time Wellman had knocked on the door. Grabbing a full bottle of whiskey, he went out the front door and met Wellman on the porch. Matthew looked down at her purse and asked her if it was her camera purse.

Wellman held up the purse and showed him the camera lens.

"Good," Matthew said with a smile. "We are going to make history today."

Matthew handed the bottle of whiskey to Wellman for safekeeping.

Matthew's car was already beaten and bruised from Mother Nature's wrath, so they hopped into his car and took off, history in the making!

As soon as they were on the highway, Wellman pulled a thermos bottle of coffee from her purse and asked Matthew if he wanted some.

"Yeah, if you add some whiskey in it," he replied.

"You know, Father, you and me think alike."

She reached into the back seat and grabbed two cups, filled them with a little coffee mixed in with a lot of whiskey and handed one to Matthew. They both sat back and relaxed, drinking their spiked coffee passing the time away with a lot of small talk. Mostly, about the two missing kids from the Costume Shop. Matthew told her what he had heard on the news. She agreed with him about keeping quiet until the time was right.

***

As the two-hour ride neared, the bottle of liquor was either half full or half empty, depending on one's point of view and the thermos of coffee was completely empty. Just as Matthew placed the bottle under his seat and simultaneously, Wellman had placed her thermos onto the floor, the phenomenon occurred once again. The Interstate disappeared and the mountain appeared in a split second nearly a nanosecond after a loud explosion of bright blinding light.

They relinquished control of their beings and car immediately the phenomenon happened. Mother Nature, however, took pity on them and only used dark swirling clouds, heavy winds and dozens and dozens of lightning bolts in very close proximity to the vehicle to either frighten them or kill them. But, as before, they made it to the other side unscathed. The spirits allowed them to drive off without any repercussions.

Along the route to the costume shop, the two investigators noticed a rather tall and large harry form walking along on their side of the road. They tried to catch up to it but it seemed the faster the vehicle went the faster the being disappeared. Whatever it was it went from a hundred feet ahead of the car to so far ahead that it disappeared in front of their eyes. By that time, they were nearing the Costume Shop and turned onto *Ghostown Lane*, the name Matthew came up with while dreaming the night before.

Once they had reached the dilapidated wooden shack that used gas for lighting, they noticed that no other cars were parked there.

"It seems there are no visitors today but us, which means we won't get a chance to record people going through that door and dying of horrendous deaths."

As they were walking up the steps of the Costume Shop, Wellman noticed Matthew's hair had turned gray overnight.

"Did you dye your hair," she asked him as they entered the shop.

He shook his head and pointed to his hair. "I woke up like this."

They looked around and saw that the place was empty.

"Hello," shouted Matthew. "Anyone here?"

Still no answer.

The two investigators were anxious to see who was taking Joker's place. When they saw the face and body of the person behind the counter they were shocked, to say the least.

When their eyes met, the first thing the little person said to Matthew was about his clothes.

"I'm sorry, sir, we don't take exchanges. You must return your costumes folded and cleaned."

Matthew took a double take after seeing this little man that supposedly had taken Joker's place. It seemed to *be* Joker. *Or* his twin brother, dressed in the exact outfit Joker had worn the day before. He was the same height and size; and had the same squinty eyes.

"Are you Joker's brother," Matthew asked him.

"I have no brother," he replied sharply.

Matthew asked him his name.

"Joker! What's yours?"

"Jack Matthew. I thought you got shot yesterday."

"I'm sorry," Joker replied, not knowing what Matthew was speaking about. "I wasn't shot yesterday or any other day.

Matthew seemed confused and looked to Wellman for an answer. She was just as confused. She had witnessed the shooting with Matthew and had no answer for the comment.

Joker spoke up and reminded Matthew about the costume. "Well, Jack Matthew, if that's one our costumes," pointing to his clothes, "you have to wear it out of the store, not into the store."

Matthew explained to Joker that he was a priest and the clothes he had on were his own and not the shops. "I mentioned this to you yesterday, but you must have forgotten."

Just then, the sound of a car door was heard and within seconds a couple came running happily into the place: Two teens probably eighteen or nineteen years of age. The male, a tall thin kid with a two-day growth of facial hair and long curly hair that hung down past his shoulders. The female that accompanied him was a beautiful long-haired blond with a knockout body and shapely legs. They looked like a couple made in heaven.

"Can I help you," Joker asked the two kids.

They quickly looked around the shop. "Yeah," said the kid with long curly hair, "if you rent out costumes."

"Where are we," asked the blond.

"Well young lady, you're standing in my costume shop," replied Joker.

As the blond was speaking with Joker, Matthew whispered to the tall thin kid. "Whatever you do, don't rent your costumes here. But if you do, just make sure you're not wearing them when you leave here."

Matthew was going to tell him more but didn't get the chance when he was interrupted by Joker.

"I heard what you were telling the kid, and if you continue I'll have to ask you to leave and not come back. You are ruining my business."

"At least I'm not ruining lives," Matthew whispered to himself.

"Did you say something?" Joker asked Matthew not able to hear what Matthew had said.

While the two kids were picking out costumes, Matthew turned and asked Wellman if she was still filming. She was, even before the phenomenon explosion.

"Keep it on the kids," ordered Matthew.

Wellman kept her purse pointed at the kids as they decided on costumes.

The kids weren't respecting the merchandise, throwing one costume after another onto the floor and stepping on them with their dirty shoes as they walked up and down the aisles.

Joker saw the chaos the kids were creating but remained silent. For the time being.

Matthew could see the anger build in Joker's face as the two kids continued destroying costumes with an air of righteousness.

As Wellman recorded the kids' every move, and while Joker watched the kids' every move, Matthew was busy digging out the spent bullet that wounded him the day before. After a few minutes, he had dug it out of the molding and put it in his jacket pocket. This was more evidence to go along with the recording.

The kids finally picked out a few different costumes. They went to the dressing room and tried on the costumes they had chosen. The first one the female tried on was a cowgirl outfit with hat, gun and boots. She pranced around the shop clicking her heals and twirling her pistol but stopped when her partner came out and showed off the costume he had picked: a Mexican bandito, with sombrero on his head, ammo belt across his chest, two holstered pistols on his hips and sandals on his feet. He was dressed as the infamous Poncho Villa. She was dressed as Belle Starr, the infamous moll of gunfighters, like Cole Younger of the famous Jesse James gang.

"Why don't people just dress up in a hobo outfit?" Matthew asked Wellman, as she filmed the two kids. "Then they wouldn't have to rent expensive costumes. You can make a hobo costume out of the rags you have at home."

Matthew wanted to keep close tabs on these two kids and not let them get too far away from his grasp. He was going to do his best to keep them from going out the door with their costumes on. He wasn't going to lose two more bodies to the spirits so he started up a conversation with Poncho, trying to get closer to them.

As Poncho was looking at other costumes, Matthew spoke up. "Nice costumes," Matthew told the kid.

"You too," replied the kid. "Are you supposed to be that priest that Bing Crosby played?"

"Oh, you mean the movie 'Going My Way!'" Matthew laughed and shook his head. "No, I am a *real* priest. I'm Father Jack Matthew."

He gave Matthew a dirty look and snapped, "I don't believe in god. I'm an atheist. The only thing I believe in is the 'green'. Money makes the world go round!"

"That's true, son," Matthew answered. "Money is the root of all evil. And there's plenty of evil going on around here."

"Are you saying I'm evil, Mister?" Poncho asked Matthew getting up into his face.

"Easy, son." Matthew backed away as not to upset the kid.

"I'm not your son!" He inched forward as Matthew continued walking back and away from the angry bandito.

Matthew was taller, bigger, heavier and weightlifter. He could put the kid out like a cigarette, but being a man of the cloth, he would leave it alone.

Even though the kid needed to learn to respect others and had a smart mouth, Matthew didn't want any harm to come to him and his significant other.

Matthew tried to calm the situation and asked the kid his name. "I'd like to know who I'm talking to. You know my name. I don't know yours."

"His name's Tommy Jacobs," interjected the kid's significant other, "and I'm Marilyn Matero."

"And I'm Father Jack Matthew. I'm glad to know you." He wanted to shake hands with the two strangers but only Marilyn shook Matthew's hand.

Matthew then introduced Wellman. "And this beautiful woman standing next to me is Janet Wellman; a good friend of mine."

Wellman reached out and shook hands with the woman, the man ignored her friendship.

Matero looked at the clothes Wellman had on and couldn't figure out the costume she was wearing.

"Who are you dressed up as?" she asked Wellman.

Wellman looked at her clothes and laughed. "Nobody sweetie. These are work clothes."

"Have you guys been here before?" Matthew asked them.

Marilyn shook her head. "No," she said. "We don't even know how we got here. We went through some strange events. Something grabbed the car and pulled us to this place. We didn't have much choice in the matter."

"Go back the way you came," Matthew warned them. "Leave this place... and without the costumes. It's detrimental to your health."

"Leave her alone," snapped Tommy. "We can decide our own fate."

"Baby, maybe we should listen to him," Marilyn begged.

"Shut up," bellowed Tommy, "and get your purse so we can pay for these costumes."

"But it's in the car."

Tommy ordered her to retrieve it from the car.

"Please don't," begged Matthew as he stood blocking the door.

The girl yelled for her man. "Tommy!"

Joker yelled at the two kids to "settle down."

Evidently, they didn't listen to him because Tommy ran past her and began pushing Matthew, trying to get him away from the door. When the two began tussling, the girl rushed Matthew and jumped on his back.

All the while, the little guy behind the counter was yelling his head off for the fighting to stop. Just at that moment, Wellman got into the mix. It was utter confusion. Wellman trying to pull the girl off Matthew, while Matthew was holding back Tommy from going out the door. But somehow Matthew lost his grip and Tommy was able to open the door. Matthew through sheer will was able to grab hold of Tommy's wrist, keeping him from going through the door and at the same time blocking the door with his body.

Tommy was about to give up, so Matthew let up a little on his hold he had on the kid and as he did, Joker was so angry with the wrestling that he came around the counter and, taking a running start and using all his might, shoved Wellman and the rest out the door and into the abyss.

"And don't come back!" Joker yelled as all four fell out the door.

Suddenly, in an instant, a nanosecond, an explosion of bright white light boomed with such force that it blew Matthew and Wellman through the air and in different directions more than fifteen feet from the Costume Shop and twenty feet away from each other. The two kids, however, didn't fare that well. They disappeared, evaporated from the explosion, including their vehicle.

Matthew's vehicle, however, was exactly where he had parked it.

Matthew and Wellman were slow to stand; after a few minutes, though, they were in each other's arms, hugging one another, maybe out of fear or just needed to feel the closeness or touch of another person to know that they were still of flesh and blood.

As they were welded to each other's bodies, they heard what sounded like hundreds of painful souls crying out for relief, for help, for freedom, but as the cries reached a feverish pitch, they suddenly diminished and then completely disappeared.

"Did you hear that?" Wellman asked Matthew.

"I did," he answered, swallowing his Adams apple.

"What happened to those kids," she asked, shaking.

"I don't really know. I do know, though, they somehow disappeared into thin air."

As Matthew walked Wellman to the car, he now knew that the Costume Shop was a stopover to the spirit world and its costumes were used to trick the unknowing traveler through the doorway and into the spirit world. The final frontier. Now Matthew had to figure a way to break that cycle.

CHAPTER 6

As Matthew and Wellman slowly got into the car, the subject of alcohol came up.

"I hate to bring it up," Wellman acknowledged, "but I'm sorer than hell and I need a swig of whiskey."

Matthew smiled and grabbed the bottle from under the seat, unscrewed the cap and handed it to Wellman. She grabbed it, like an addict grabbing a syringe full of liquid dreams to shove in his vein, and took two big swigs of *her* liquid dreams. She passed it to Matthew with a sigh of relief. For the next few minutes, they passed the bottle back and forth until both were numb and could feel no pain.

Matthew then drove away. Just before they reached the mountain Matthew was able to stash the bottle and what was left in it under the seat just as the *force* took control and forced the car up and up until it reached its peak.

Mother Nature must have been napping because the wind, rain, hail and lightning never materialized. But as the car began falling, something pushed the car forward at an incredible speed, never this fast in the past, something unexpected was occurring. The G-force on their bodies was overwhelming, so much so that it left impressions or indentations in the seats.

As they were nearing the bottom, one giant whoosh, sent the vehicle flying into the air, just as the mountain disappeared and the Interstate reappeared. Times before, coming out of this Matthew nearly hit a car, and more than once. He got lucky on those particular days. On this one, though, his luck finally ran out.

Just as Matthew's car was coming in for a landing, another was just passing. At that exact moment, Matthew turned the steering wheel and sideswiped the car. But it wasn't just any car; it was a police car, with two angry policemen inside.

Matthew had crashed into the passenger side of the car, putting numerous scratches and dents on both doors, but luckily not doing that much damage. Still, the cops weren't happy campers. And the two spirit busters would learn that sooner rather than later.

The cars slowed to a stop as the cop car flashed its lights and blew its siren behind Matthew's car. Matthew pulled the car over to the side of the road and ordered Wellman to stay silent.

"Let me do all the talking," he told her, while they waited for the cops to make their presence.

As the cops came up on each side of the vehicle with weapons drawn, the cop on the driver's side was a little shocked at seeing a priest behind the wheel. He was even more shocked when Matthew spoke to him through his open window.

"Father, have you been drinking?" the fat cop asked him.

"I can explain. I…"

Before Matthew could speak another word, the cop had him step out of the car. "Get out of the car, Father. And put your hands on top of the car."

"But I can explain, Officer," Matthew whined. "If you'd just give me the chance. I'm working in conjunction with the State police. The woman inside my car is Detective Janet Wellman. We're working on Senator Strang's Missing Person's investigation and others. Just radio Captain Bird. He can verify my story."

"He can," blurted Wellman.

The cop bent down and looked at Wellman through the window. "Ma'am, you want to step out of the car and my partner will check your identification and make sure you're not carrying any weapons on your person."

As Wellman stepped out of the car, she set the two cops straight. "Listen, guys. Of course, I have a weapon. I'm a Detective with the State Police."

"Ma'am," said the skinny cop, frisking Wellman, "be quiet until we make sure our lives aren't in any danger. Where's your identification?"

She told him it was in her purse that was sitting on the front seat of the car. "But please be careful. It's a camera purse."

The cop grabbed the purse out of the car and rummaged through it, finding her thirty-eight caliber pistol, identification and the camera inside the purse.

"What's the camera for?" he asked her.

"For taking pictures," she replied, sarcastically.

"I don't think you're in a position to cop an attitude," he told her.

He finished the frisk and had her turn around to face him and answer questions, while he looked at her identification. He flipped open her wallet and saw her badge and police identification.

"You're Detective Janet Wellman. I guess you are who you say you are."

As the cop placed the wallet into the purse, his nose was close enough to Wellman to smell her breath. And he smelled alcohol on her. "Have you been drinking?" he asked her, looking directly into her eyes.

While the cop was questioning Wellman about her drinking, Matthew was busy taking a breathalyzer test. He failed miserably. "Father, your alcoholic intake is three times the legal limit," said the cop, as he cuffed Matthew and walked him back to his squad car.

Soon afterward, Wellman was given a number of tests for alcohol inebriation, including the breathalyzer. She also failed all the tests, like her partner. The officer placed her hands behind her back and handcuffed her, then walked her to the squad car and placed her next to Matthew. Before the cop closed the door, Wellman begged him to take her back to her precinct.

"We have some very important evidence on Senator Strang's disappearance. We need to speak to Captain Bird now. Please, I beg you," she whined.

The cop could see the agony in her eyes.

"She's telling the truth, sir," interjected Matthew.

"I'll get back with you," he told them as he closed the door, then walked over to speak with his partner.

The two cops talked over the situation and decided to ask them a few more pertinent questions before deciding the outcome. They walked back to the car and opened the rear door to speak with both collars. They would question each one separately, separated by the car. The fat one questioned Matthew while the tall and thin one questioned Wellman.

"Now, Ma'am, what is so important that you guys came out of nowhere like a ***bat out of hell*** and sideswiped a police car for Christ sake."

"You're right about coming out of nowhere," she said, sarcastically. She gave out a sickly laugh.

"Why have you been drinking?"

"You won't believe me if I told you."

"Try me!"

"We've been drinking after seeing some unbelievable *things*."

"What kind of *things*?"

"The Legend of Hollow Pass *things*. You heard of that, haven't you, Officer?"

"Are you kidding? You saw demons and spirits?"

"Well, no. But we went to a place that supposedly doesn't exist in the real world, only in the spirit world."

"I think I've heard enough!"

The fat cop was basically told the same story by Matthew.

The cops placed the two back into the squad car, then talked among themselves deciding on a happy or sad ending.

"What are we going to do with them?" asked the fat cop. "I mean the woman is a detective with the State Police."

"And the guy's a priest. So, what?" barked the thin cop.

"I'm just saying, we should show them a curtesy and take them back to their precinct and let their captain discipline them."

"But they're both drunk," he reminded his partner, "and they smashed into our car. We should make an example of them and show that we don't care who the person is. If they're driving under the influence, then they need to be arrested and taken to jail. Period."

"I'm sorry, but I say we take them to their precinct and let their captain discipline them. If he wants to charge them, then so be it. What do you say?"

The skinny cop thought it over and decided that his partner had more seniority so he agreed with him. He figured that if **they** got balled out by **their** superiors, he could always blame the situation on his partner.

"What do we do with their car?" asked the skinny cop.

The fat cop thought about a solution to the problem for nearly thirty seconds before coming up with an answer. He snapped his finger and cried out, "I got it! You drive their car and I'll drive them in the squad car. They can tell their ridiculous story to their superiors."

So the two cops got into their respective cars and started for the State Police precinct where Wellman worked. The squad car took off first and Matthew's car followed.

Wellman was curious and asked the fat cop exactly where he was taking them.

"Just sit back and relax," he answered.

"Are you taking us back to our precinct?" she asked him.

"Detective, please, just sit back and relax."

"Janet," interjected Matthew, "it's no use. Wherever we're going our lives are ruined. When the Church hears about this, I'm finished. They'll excommunicate me."

Wellman figured at the very least, she would be fired from her profession, if not jailed. She agreed with Matthew and gave up her begging, and finally relaxed, bowing to her fate.

This was the longest ride the two investigators had ever taken. By the time they had arrived in the precinct's parking lot, Wellman and Matthew were snuggling against one another when they were taken out of the squad car and their cuffs removed.

"Let's see how your boss reacts to your explanation," said the fat cop.

Matthew and Wellman walked into the station very uneasy to say the least. At that time, the thin cop handed Wellman's purse and its contents to her and the fat cop returned Matthew's holy water to him.

"Show us to your superior's office," said the fat cop to Wellman.

When they got to the door of Captain Bird's office they had to wait there because Bird was busy speaking with five leaders of the community, which were three religious leaders, the mayor and the deputy mayor.

As the four stood outside the door of Bird's office, they started up a conversation as to what Wellman was going to tell her Captain. Wellman had a simple answer.

"I'll tell him the truth," she answered. "As crazy as it'll sound, but I'll say it like it is because I have the proof right here in my purse that the Legend is no more. It is now a reality and Father Matthew and I have proved the Legend of Hollow Pass actually exists."

While Wellman was telling all that could hear the story that Matthew and her had witnessed, one person that didn't like what she had to say was the jealous Carolyn Hampton.

Hampton walked up to Wellman and confronted her. "I should have been the one that helped Jack, not you," she said angrily.

Matthew spoke up and defended Wellman. "Carolyn, you aren't a descendant and she is. The spirits wouldn't let you enter their realm. They don't want you. So you should feel lucky that you didn't have to go through what Janet and I saw today."

Carolyn didn't want to hear any excuses. She was in love with Father Jack Matthew and would do anything to get Wellman away from him. As she stood there fuming, Wellman tried to calm Hampton down but Hampton would have none of it and flipped out. She grabbed Wellman's purse that held the evidence to the Legend, threw it on the ground and stomped on it and the camera inside before anyone could stop her.

As the fat cop held onto Hampton so she couldn't do anymore damage, Hampton yelled words of anger at Wellman. "Jack loves *me*, not you." She squirmed out of the cop's firm grip and walked back to her desk crying.

Captain Bird saw the commotion outside his office and so did the leaders, including one who was Bishop Mike Cullity, Matthew's Boss. Both he and Matthew noticed each other at about the same time. At that moment Matthew prayed that god would make him disappear or invisible just for the immediate future, but evidently god didn't hear his prayer. Matthew was still visible and given the *look of the devil* from his boss.

Captain Bird came out from his office with a vengeance and yelled, "What the hell is going on out here." He looked at Wellman. "And what the hell are you doing here? You called in sick."

"Yes, sir, I can explain," she said biting her lip, then picked up her purse off the floor.

Bird suddenly noticed the two officers. "And what are these two officers doing here?" He looked to them for an answer.

The fat cop answered Bird's question. "I'm Officer Charles Lamb," then pointing to his skinny partner, added, "And this is my partner, Officer George Cronk. Can we go into your office and talk? I think we need to explain the situation to you in private."

"Okay, but give me a few minutes to say goodbye to my guests."

Bird stepped back into his office and cut his meeting short with the leaders of the city. "I'm sorry, gentlemen, but something's come up and it needs immediate attention. Please forgive me, but it can't be helped." He watched as the five left the room.

As the men passed those who were involved in the escapade, Matthew and Cullity's eyes met and the Bishop stopped to say a few words to the priest.

"Father Matthew, I see that you're still having problems. I will give you a call tomorrow and set up a meeting with you. We need to talk."

Matthew nodded, sweat pouring off his face as the alcohol seeped out of his pores. The Bishop noticed as he walked away with the others.

As the leaders walked away, Bird invited Wellman, Matthew and the two cops into his office.

"Please, take a seat," Bird told the four.

They took their seats.

Bird wanted answers and started with the cops. "So why are you guys here with my investigators," he asked Officer Lamb.

Lamb, playing with his hat, finally answered him. "Well, sir, the Father sideswiped our car on I-5. They came out of nowhere and hit us. When we questioned them, they were both under the influence of alcohol."

"They were soused," interjected Cronk.

Lamb "shushed" his partner and continued explaining. "Sir."

"It's Captain Bird," he told them.

"Well, Captain," continued Lamb, "when we found out Miss Wellman was a detective within your department, we decided against taking them to our precinct where we would have had to book them into the jail, which, most likely, would have ruined their lives. So, we decided to do the right thing and bring them here so you could discipline your people. I hope we did the right thing."

Bird agreed and thanked them. "Thank you, gentlemen."

The two cops shook Bird's hand. "I wouldn't be too harsh with them," said Officer Lamb.

Bird told them that Wellman was under his authority and would be dealt with immediately. He looked at Matthew. "Father Matthew, however, isn't, but I believe Bishop Cullity will deal with him."

"Oh, I'm sure he will," muttered Matthew under his breath.

Bird thanked the officers again. Before leaving, Officer Cronk handed Matthew's car keys to him. Matthew thanked him halfheartedly.

Once the two cops had left the room, Bird lit in on his two troublemakers.

"So, let me see if I got this straight," he said, sarcastically, looking directly into Wellman's eyes. "First of all, Wellman, you should be home in bed. You called in sick. Remember?"

"That was my fault," Matthew blurted.

Bird became somewhat enraged and turned his attention to Matthew. "This whole damn thing sounds like it's your fault," bellowed Bird.

"But Captain, let me explain," whined Wellman.

Bird told her not to say another word. "I'm asking the questions."

The two investigators sat silent as Bird asked away. "First of all, Father, I want to know why in the hell you were driving drunk and putting lives in danger? You're lucky you're not sitting behind bars right now." He looked at Wellman. "And that goes for you too!"

"Sir," whined Wellman, "if you'd just let me explain."

Bird would have none of it and held up his hand to stop her from speaking. To put it mildly, he was upset and angry, to say the very least.

He looked to Matthew again. "And I told you, Father, that I had a replacement for Wellman to help with your father's investigation. I went out of my way to help you and not hinder you and then this happens."

"But Captain Bird, we had no control of the situation," exclaimed Matthew.

Bird gave out a nervous laugh. "So you're telling me that someone poured alcohol down your throat. I don't think so."

"I'm not saying that at all," replied Matthew.

"Then what are you saying, Father?"

"Maybe I can explain it better, Captain," interjected Wellman.

"Oh, I can't wait to hear it."

Wellman gave it her best shot. "Sir, both Father Matthew and I are descendants of the killers that massacred that Indian village at Hollow Pass back in the eighteen sixties."

"Wellman, you're drunk and talking nonsense. If you're going to tell me that the Legend of Hollow Pass is the reason and excuse for your drunkenness and recklessness, it isn't going to work."

"Captain, we witnessed and filmed a young couple disappearing through some sort of vortex. That's not all. We could hear the victims that were imprisoned for all eternity in some type of black hole."

"Wellman," Bird barked, "are you listening to yourself? Do you know how crazy you sound? 'Listening to victims imprisoned in a black hole.' You better watch yourself with that kind of talk or you may end up in that insane asylum up the street."

"But Captain," she whined, "we have some extraordinary evidence. I have the proof here in my purse that the Legend does exist." She grabbed the camera from inside her purse and pulled out a number of pieces. It was shattered and broken. Hampton had really done a job by destroying everything that was in the purse.

When Wellman and Matthew saw the damage, they were disgusted and dumbfounded. They were at a loss for words. Then Matthew remembered the SIM card.

"Janet, check the SIM card. See if that's still intact. We can use it in another camera to show the film."

She quickly checked for the card but that too was destroyed, broken in three little pieces. The two investigators were even more distraught now after seeing all their hard work and evidence go down the tubes. Even though Matthew was a priest and Wellman, a missing person's detective, nobody would believe their story without reliable and pertinent evidence, especially when it involved the Legend of Hollow Pass.

She gave Bird a dejected look and said, "I'm sorry, sir, our evidence was destroyed when Hampton stomped on my purse. And I know she did it on purpose. That bitch!"

"That's enough of that, Janet," snapped Bird. "Maybe your evidence disappeared in a black hole." Bird let out a chuckle, then was serious again. "The Legend of Hollow Pass. You know how I feel on that subject. And you and Hampton fighting like two little school girls. I don't know what to do with you."

"Captain, Hampton's in love with Father Matthew," she explained. "She thinks I'm taking him away from her. Hampton's delusional."

"What about it, Father? Is that true?"

"Yes, sir. I'm afraid it is. I've done everything in my power to ignore her advances. I've explained to her more than once that I'm a man of the Church. She just can't get it through her head. I thought she would get over her infatuation with me when we went our separate ways, but she hasn't. And for some reason Hampton became extremely jealous of Wellman. I have no idea, why? But she is."

Bird's thoughts returned to his detective. "Wellman, you have only yourself to blame for the trouble you're in. And you've given me one big headache. I could site you for drunk and disorderly or a number of other charges. How should I discipline you? And Hampton? All this nonsense going on during Senator Strang's investigation. I'm going to have to think long and hard on what action needs to be taken. Had I been those cops, I'd have locked both of you up. Period!"

Then Bird turned his attention to Matthew. "And you, Father. Driving while intoxicated and causing an accident. I would have thought that you would have been the rational one between the two of you, but I see now that you're just as reckless. This does not sit well with me and I'm sure it won't sit well with Bishop Cullity. You know I will have to call him about your actions. And if I tell him about this exorcism or whatever it is you're doing investigating this crazy notion that the Legend of Hollow Pass exists, I don't think he'll think too highly of what you're doing. But you'll have to take that up with him. Right now, I want the both of you to get out of my office and go home. I'll deal with you two tomorrow. Right now, I have some fence mending to do."

As the two were leaving, Bird had one thing left to say to Matthew. "Oh, Father, Wellman's replacement will be here in the morning, so if you're still adamant about investigating your father's disappearance, you can see her then. Whether she's a descendant of the killers or not I don't know. I guess you'll have to ask her." Bird let out a hysterical laugh over his sarcasm.

Matthew and Wellman continued their trek out of the office and headed towards the precinct's front doors.

Hampton seeing them together hurried after them, waving her hands and shouting, "Wait, Jack. Wait for me. I need to speak with you."

Standing at the front doors, Matthew turned and scolded her. "Carolyn, you've done enough damage for one day. You've destroyed the most important proof ever collected on the Legend of Hollow Pass. Now, leave me alone, leave Janet alone and get yourself some psychological help. I really mean that."

With that said, Matthew and Wellman left the building and headed for their cars. Hampton followed after them but was called back by Captain Bird.

"Carolyn, get in here, we need to talk," he said in frustration.

She turned and headed into the building. She followed Bird into his office.

"Take a seat, Carolyn," said Bird as he took his seat.

*****

While Carolyn was waiting to hear what Bird had to say, Matthew and Wellman were hatching a plan to continue their quest in their search for evidence to show that the Legend does exist, even to this day, and to get those agonizing voices out of limbo and out of the void in which they were in.

As the two were walking to their vehicles, Matthew told Wellman to meet him at his place. "Follow me. We have to figure out a different course of action, just in case nobody is there to go through that door. But we have to go back there again, later today. And we need another recording device. Can you get one?" he asked her.

She said she could. "Give me an hour. I have to borrow another camera. I'll come over afterwards."

The two hopped into their cars and sped away in different directions, just in case someone was watching them.

Matthew drove home feeling that he was being followed. "But why?" He thought to himself. "And who would be following him?" His paranoia turned passive when he came up with an answer. Matthew figured it was someone from the precinct making sure he arrived home safely. He noticed, though, that the car had followed him all the way to his place, then drove past, made a U-turn and parked just across and a few houses down from his place.

Matthew ignored their presence. He was concerned only with drinking and getting into his home as quickly as possible so he could begin exercising his arm.

CHAPTER 7

Matthew and Wellman were still planning to work together, even after Wellman had been ordered, not once, but twice, not to work with Matthew, but she defied her boss's commands. She felt she had no other choice. The outcome, if not planned and carried out correctly, could have dire consequences on the area for generations to come.

Hampton, on the other hand, was sitting in front of her boss waiting to be chewed out. And he gave it to her with both barrels.

"Carolyn, what has gotten into you lately? You're acting like a little school girl who has a crush on a teacher. You're not thinking rationally. I think you need some time off. So, take a few days off. Don't come back until your head's screwed on straight. Get me!"

She nodded.

"What? I didn't hear you," Bird barked.

"Yes, sir. I understand."

"Now, get out of my sight!"

Hampton, feeling the sting of Bird's wrath, slowly stood up and walked slowly and dejectedly out of his office. Within five minutes she had left the precinct as Bird had ordered. But she wasn't going home directly as Bird had ordered. She was going to drive to a bar and have a few drinks to wallow in her sorrow and then, when she had built up enough courage, she would drive to Matthew's home to speak with him concerning their love life.

***

The first thing Matthew did when he entered his abode was to do what he had done every day: go into the kitchen, grab the whiskey bottle and glass, then go into the living room, plop his butt onto the couch and drink until he had enough alcohol in him so he could think, otherwise his anxiety and nervousness would take control of his body.

Once he had filled his glass, he grabbed his remote and turned on the television to a news channel. Ten minutes into the program he was surprised at what he heard. What did he hear, but two names that he had heard only hours before: Tommy Jacobs and Marilyn Matero.

"But how could anyone know so soon that these two kids were missing?" he thought to himself.

Neither Matthew nor Wellman mentioned any names of the kids to anyone. He wondered who could have told the news station about this new revelation.

As he searched the file cabinet in his brain, he couldn't think of anyone that could have known that information but Wellman. And he didn't believe it was her. He had just talked with her an hour before in the precinct parking lot.

He took another shot of whiskey and decided to wait for her visit and ask her about the news story. He didn't have to wait too long.

***

Less than an hour had passed since leaving the precinct's parking lot when Matthew heard a knock on the door. He opened it and was happy to see Wellman with another, what looked like a camera purse on her arm.

"Come in." He invited her in for a drink or two before leaving for a second try at exposing the Legend once and for all.

This time they would make sure nothing happened to their evidence by staying far away from Hampton; and Bird for that matter.

The two went into the living and sat together on the couch.

Matthew poured them each a double shot of whiskey which they downed like troopers. "Alright, let's get down to work." He looked down at Wellman's lap and focused in on the camera purse. "Now does that camera purse work?" When she didn't answer fast enough, he asked her again, "It is a camera purse, isn't it?"

"Yes, here take a look," she said, handing him the purse, while leaning against him.

While he was looking at the purse, Wellman grabbed the bottle of whiskey and poured them each another double shot. She handed one to Matthew and made a toast.

"To us!" They clinked their glasses together and chugged their shots.

Suddenly, the news story about the two missing young adults was playing, their names mentioned.

Wellman heard the names and looked at Matthew. "Let me explain," she whined.

When Matthew heard those words come out of her mouth he now knew who the guilty party was. "What did you do?" he asked her.

"I had to get the story out. So, I went to my connection at the local news station. We had to let the people know that those two kids didn't disappear for nothing. We have to turn these naysayers into believers. Just like you were in the beginning. You didn't believe in the Legend. And now you're ready to do whatever it takes to defeat the power that controls that ghost town and its freak of nature. We know what happened to those kids, now everyone else knows too. I made the right decision."

"I just wish you hadn't done it without my input. You could have told me that you were going to do that."

"Well, it's over with now."

Wellman grabbed the bottle again and began pouring Matthew another shot while he was holding the glass and missed, pouring whiskey all over his shirt. She set the bottle down on the table and apologized for being so clumsy.

Matthew didn't say a word. He remained calm and took off his shirt with help from Wellman. Then they noticed that his pants were also wet. Before Matthew could go into his bedroom and change into another shirt and pair of pants, Wellman was busy tearing his pants off his body.

But a knock on the door, interrupted her endeavor. Matthew began walking towards his bedroom when he stopped dead in his tracks in the hallway leading to the front door. He was surprised to see Carolyn Hampton standing in his foyer, and Hampton was surprised to see him nearly naked, with only his underwear and socks covering his body. He ran back into the living room to put his wet clothes on.

"I knocked but nobody answered," she said as she followed Matthew.

Hampton had a smile on her face as she entered the living room but her face turned from a picture of happiness to one of sheer rage when she saw Wellman kneeling on the floor, Matthew standing near her and a half-empty bottle of whiskey and two full shot glasses sitting on the table nearby.

Hampton believed she had interrupted their party and sexual rendezvous. She literally went berserk, tipping over furniture, breaking knick-knacks, just anything that was within her reach.

Matthew tried to calm her down. "It's nothing, Carolyn. I just spilled whiskey all over my clothes and Janet was cleaning up the mess."

That excuse seemed to make things worse. Hampton spewed foul language and curse words at the two, as Matthew and Wellman sat down on the couch and allowed her to get whatever was on her mind off her chest.

Matthew grabbed his clothes off the floor and tried to use them to cover himself while Hampton continued with her tirade.

With all the shouting and yelling coming out of Hampton's mouth, nobody noticed another person had entered the house through the open front door that Hampton never closed, and followed the noise leading into the living room. All were shocked at the person who was standing in the entranceway, especially Matthew.

"Bishop Cullity," Matthew shouted, as he stood up, holding his loose clothes against his body, trying to hide his nakedness.

"Father Matthew," bellowed the Bishop, "what is going on in this… this… den of inequity?"

"I can explain, Bishop."

"Enough!" he shouted.

The Bishop looked at the ladies and asked them to leave. "I have to speak with Father Matthew."

The two women couldn't get out of there fast enough and all the while bickering and arguing with each other over Father Matthew.

With the women gone, Cullity and Matthews were able to talk. Well, at least Cullity was able to talk. Matthew was too busy getting chewed out, while putting on his wet and smelly clothes, which the Bishop noticed had the smell of alcohol. The Bishop gave it to him with both barrels, then reloaded and gave it to him again.

"What has happened to you, Jack? You used to be one of our best and brightest. Now this!" He pointed to Matthew's nakedness.

"Sir, why are you here?" Matthew asked him.

He soon learned the answer.

It seemed Captain Bird was true to his word and had contacted Bishop Cullity, explaining Matthew's situation to him concerning the broads, booze and his sanity. Now the Bishop was here to call him out on it.

Cullity continued. "I came here hoping what Captain Bird had told me wasn't true. But what did I find? You, drunk and naked... with two women hanging all over you. It looked to me as if you were about to have a threesome."

Matthew begged to be heard. "Please, Bishop Cullity, let me explain. I can explain."

Cullity didn't want to hear what he had to say. It was Matthew's turn to listen.

"And what is this that I'm hearing that you're investigating that crazy legend. The Legend of Hollow Pass, I believe is what it's called."

Matthew nodded. "That's what it's called," he said under his breath.

"So is it true? Are you really trying to prove that the legend really exists?"

Matthew nodded. "If you'll just hear me out."

"That's ridiculous. I just don't know what the Church will do with you. The Vatican suspended you from your work for alcoholism, so you come back here for rehabilitation… and I see now that rehab has not worked. You are drinking more now than ever before. What is the problem, Father Matthew?"

Cullity just shook his head in disgust as he loomed over a sitting Matthew and stared straight through him. He tried to wipe out the evil that had consumed Matthew's body using his piercing eyes.

"I hope you remember that it was I who ordained you in the Order of Melchisideck. I, who was your mentor in every sense of the word. Now it will be up to me and the board to decide your fate."

Matthew tried his hardest to change Cullity's mind. "Sir, I know you may think it's crazy, but I have been to Hollow Pass. I and one of the ladies that just left have witnessed people disappear into some sort of vortex. But in order to get there, I've proven that you have to be a descendant of someone who was involved with the massacre of the Indian village of Hollow Pass back in the eighteen-sixties."

Before he said another word, Cullity jumped back into the conversation. "Jack, are you serious? Are you listening to yourself? You sound looney tunes. I think you may need a mental checkup. I've heard it all now, and coming from one of the Church's prize possessions. Jack, you ought to be ashamed of yourself."

"Bishop Cullity, everything I've told you is gospel. Not only do I believe in the Legend but I believe the souls those spirits and demons are taking are in a state of limbo, kind of like in a black hole. Wellman and I heard their painful screams when we saw those two kids disappear. In fact, their names were read on a news show today and we just witnessed their disappearances just a few hours ago. The police haven't even listed them as 'missing persons' yet. But we know that they ***will be*** by tomorrow."

"You actually think that spirits and demons are really taking living people and exchanging their souls for the souls of the dead Indians? Is that what you're saying, Jack?"

"That's exactly what I'm saying, Mike, and I believe I've come up with a sound plan to release those people from their torment of painful non-existence."

"Just listen to yourself. You have lost it. I think all that alcohol you've consumed over the years has had an adverse effect on you. Get it together and get sober. Or else."

Matthew tried a different approach to get his point across. "Bishop Cullity, we believe in god and we can't see or feel him. But we know he's everywhere you look. And I've seen and heard similar voices and visions during the exorcism's that I've participated in for the Vatican. The Church believes in that. But we can't believe in these particular spirits that are taking loved ones from this area for loved ones that were lost back in the eighteen-sixties. And I believe I can unlock that door that holds back all those victims from escaping back to their particular reality."

"I give up," said Bishop Cullity, disgusted and dumbfounded by Father Matthew's words. "I give you warning now. Straighten up your life now... or we'll have to excommunicate you from the Church. I will have to call a meeting with my superiors and board and figure out how to deal with your problem correctly. The Church has put a lot of time and money into you and your studies. We'd hate to see it go to waste, but that's exactly what will happen if you do not heed my words."

Matthew stayed silent but pleaded his case with his puppy-love eyes. That, however, didn't work.

Before Bishop Cullity left Matthew's home, he had one last thing to say to Matthew. "You don't do anything tomorrow. I want you to wait for my phone call. I'll let you know the time of the meeting. We've got to get your thoughts about the Legend of Hollow Pass out of your head and get your head back to thinking about god and the Church. It's your last chance."

With that, Bishop Cullity left Matthew's home in an angry mood. He had had enough of Father Matthew's foolishness.

Did Matthew heed Bishop Cullity's words of sobriety? No! As soon as Cullity was out the door, Matthew grabbed the half-empty bottle of whiskey, filled the glass and chugged it; then a second and a third. He was disgruntled and saddened by the fact that nobody believed him or Wellman concerning what each had witnessed.

***

Matthew sat on that couch until the bottle was empty. Soon after, he got up and went into his bedroom to finally change out of his whiskey smelling clothes and into fresh and clean ones. With that done, he went into the kitchen and grabbed another bottle of whiskey, then headed towards the living room and his comfortable couch but was stopped in his tracks when he heard a knock on the door. He froze. He thought maybe it was Bishop Cullity again and he was much drunker now than earlier. He almost didn't open it. He was fearful of the outcome. But he finally got up the nerve, took a deep breath and opened the door, only to see standing there was Janet Wellman carrying her camera purse.

"Janet, come in," Matthew said as he stumbled into the living room and planted his behind onto his couch.

She followed and sat next to him, then grabbed the bottle out of his hand and poured herself a drink but didn't pour one for Matthew. "You look like you don't need a drink right now, especially if we're going to Hollow Pass." She chugged her drink and poured another, then looked to Matthew. "So, are we going or what?"

Matthew didn't answer right away. He was in an alcoholic daze. "What?" he asked.

"Are we going to Hollow Pass? We should get going if we are. Remember, it's a two-hour drive."

She leaned against him trying to put some life into the party. Matthew, however, wasn't in the mood. He was only thinking about tomorrow's meeting with the board members of the Church and his excommunication, if that is what they so desired.

"Pour me a drink," he said to Wellman.

She poured him a drink and gave it to him, then picked up her glass and drank with him.

Matthew finished his drink and set it on the table then turned to Wellman and told her something she wasn't ready to hear. "I'm sorry, Janet, but I can't gather more evidence today. Bishop Cullity has ordered me to severe my ties with you and my quest to bring those souls back to their homes."

Wellman tried to reason with him. "Captain Bird ordered me not to work with you but I did anyway. This is bigger than the both of us. We have to do it. We've been to that place twice and we're still in good shape, except for your hair turning gray and maybe a few more wrinkles. I noticed some changes to my body too. It must be the alcohol finally catching up with me. But we can't stop now." She pleaded with him.

Matthew would have none of it. He was still a man of the cloth and once, had high-standing in the Church. Now he wanted to work his way back to that high standard. But his demons were winning, taking the fight out of him to overcome his alcohol addiction. He was hoping that if he could fight and defeat those demons and spirits that were haunting Hollow Pass, he would have a better feel when fighting the demons within his body. It might even help him fight and cast out the demons in his exorcisms. It was a win-win for Matthew. Bishop Cullity, however, didn't see it that way. And right now, he was Matthew's boss and savior, but only if Matthew took his words to heart. So, he had to be on his best behavior and turned down Wellman's request.

Their drinking got the best of them and they fell asleep where they sat for nearly four hours before getting up.

Wellman made them supper and the two ate a meal of spaghetti, washed down with lots of coffee.

It was getting late so Matthew offered Wellman his guest bedroom so she wouldn't have to drive home so late.

She took him up on his offer and after the meal they returned to the living room to watch television before going to bed. Wellman had no nightgown or pajamas so Matthew gave her a pair of his pajamas and a Vatican robe. He also changed into the same garb. A few hours later, they were dead to the world and sleeping like babies. Well one of them anyway.

Matthew was having trouble with nightmares. Three hours after nodding off, he awoke sopping wet, not just his pajamas but also the sheets, and all because he had the same nightmare he had twenty-four hours before. He perspired so much you would have thought he wet the bed. He changed into dry pajamas and then changed the sheets before getting back into bed. He took a few deep breaths and within a few minutes was sawing logs.

Not long after, Matthew was awakened again from that same nightmare: fireballs spewing out of Joker's mouth and landing on his body, burning it to a crisp, leaving him to die an agonizing death—burned alive. The burned body suddenly turned into ash, which fell to the floor and formed three words: *jump thru door.* Nearly the same exact dream he had just hours before, with the same effect on his body.

Looking at the clock, he noticed it was still very early but he decided to stay up. He walked into the kitchen and made himself some coffee.

As he was waiting for the coffee to percolate he walked into the living room to check on Wellman. She was still sleeping. He called out her name, but no answer. She was dead to the world. He let her sleep another hour before waking her. He offered her coffee, which she happily accepted. She sat up and Matthew sat next to her.

As the two were drinking their coffee a knock on the door was heard. Matthew stood to answer it, but the person knocking had already let himself in.

Matthew was embarrassed and in shock at seeing who the person standing there was. It was Bishop Cullity. He came to pick up Matthew and drive him to the board meeting.

Cullity, however, was, to say the least, aghast at the picture in front of him: Matthew, and Wellman, a woman he was ordered to stay away from, were both in the living room in their pajamas and robes. Cullity could only theorize about the sexual connotation that he was now witnessing. He was outraged and ordered Matthew to dress.

He looked at Wellman. "And I'd advise you to do the same, Miss," he told her.

Both Matthew and Wellman remained silent throughout their ordeal with the Bishop.

Wellman went into the bathroom to change into her clothes and when she was finished she walked slowly out the door, to her car and then drove away.

Matthew had dressed soon after Wellman and met with Bishop Cullity, following him to his limo. While getting into it, he noticed the car that had followed him and parked across the street the day before was still there with two men inside. "Why?" he wondered.

"Where are we headed?" Matthew asked Cullity.

Cullity looked at him with questioning eyes. "To see what your future holds!" replied Cullity.

CHAPTER 8

The two men of the cloth had few words to say as they rode in Bishop Cullity's limo to the church. After being dropped off, they walked up the fifty-two stairs and went inside, bypassing the alter and walking straight into the conference room where eight men, six in Catholic robes, the other two in suits, all in their sixties or older, were all sitting in big chairs around a giant table. There was no small talk or conversation. They sat silently in their seats and waited patiently to see and speak with Father Matthew.

Once Cullity and Matthew had taken their seats, the eight men suddenly came to life and the meeting got underway. Bishop Cullity started it off by introducing Father Matthew to everyone sitting at the table. They were nice to him to that point. From that point on, though, the meeting took a serious turn.

Bishop Cullity continued. "Gentlemen, we are here today to see if Father Matthew still has a future with the Church. As you know, he has been on suspension from his work at the Vatican because alcohol had taken over his willpower. And he has yet to overcome those demons within him that are usurping his power. Gentlemen, to put it mildly, Father Matthew has been flirting with the devil. He is being pursued by not one, but two women of possibly ill repute."

Father Matthew couldn't listen to this tripe without standing up for himself. "Those women were missing persons' detectives. They were not women of ill repute. Bishop Cullity, I resent the accusation."

Cullity shot back. "Then you admit that those two women of which I speak… are pursuing you. Is that right?"

"I'm sorry. It's not like that. If I can explain," Matthew begged.

Cullity would have none of it. He was asking the questions and explaining the situation to the men who would decide Matthew's future with the Church. That is, if he still had one.

"Is it not true, Father Matthew, that I caught you yesterday with two women who were fighting over you and then today, I find you with one of the same woman both you and she in bathrobes. Are you going to deny that, Father?"

Matthew looked down to the floor and could only nod. Then he started to fight back. "Yes, that's true, but…"

Cullity cut him off with a swipe of his hand. "I am not finished, Father," acknowledged Cullity. "Didn't I also find you drunk and smelling of alcohol, yesterday and today? And drinking with those women? A bottle of whiskey on the table in front of you… and with only your underwear on? Tell the men at this table if I'm lying. Am I lying, Father Matthew?"

Matthew was definitely agitated by the accusations being thrown his way, but was unable to defend himself. Bishop Cullity wouldn't allow him to give his side of the story. Matthew wasn't giving up though. He would wait until the time was right and speak his peace. But right at that particular moment, all Matthew could do was, once again, just give a nod.

"You don't have anything to say?" Cullity asked him.

"May I speak, Bishop Cullity, without being interrupted?" Matthew answered.

Cullity wanted to deny him the opportunity, but the others in the room had other ideas. "Let him speak," said one of the men wearing robes. "I want to hear what he has to say."

The others around the table seconded the motion.

Matthew cleared his throat and began giving his explanation. "First, let me say, yes, it's true I was suspended for alcoholism and yes it's true that I'm still fighting my demons and yes it's true that I have two women who are infatuated with me, but that's all it is, it's an infatuation. Many of you here sitting at the table I'm sure have had similar women infatuated with you."

Many nodded at Matthew's comment. Other's had no feelings on the subject.

Matthew continued. "But no matter, I'm a man of the cloth; a man of the Church. Women have no place in my life. I try to console them, to comfort them when they're in need. That's it. Nothing more goes on. But I will admit, my drinking does not help the situation."

"Okay, enough of that," interjected Cullity. "Tell the men sitting at this table what you know about the Legend of Hollow Pass. Tell them what you told me." Cullity looked at the men. "You have to hear this," he added.

Matthew began his story about Hollow Pass. "Well, it actually started years ago when my father, who had been a homicide detective, was investigating his partner's disappearance. Soon after, my father ended up as a missing person investigation. The case was closed when the *powers that be* decided my father had absconded with a younger woman and started a new life. I didn't believe it and when I returned home, I began my own investigation, which took me to a place like no other. It took me to a waystation, a stopover, a little shack called the Costume Shop, sitting alone in a ghost town. This place I'm talking about is a time warp in space, a portal, an opening where certain people are drawn in and taken by the Indian spirits or some say, the Indian gods. But no matter, this is an evil place, in an evil time, in a fourth dimension and we must rid all evil from the face of this earth. And I believe I can do just that."

The room was completely silent. Not a sound heard. Then one of the men dressed in a suit spoke up.

"So, you believe that this evil place isn't hell but a fourth dimension, a portal to the afterlife? Is that what you're saying, Father Matthew."

"Yes. I witnessed this myself, along with Detective Wellman. We had the evidence until one of the women that Bishop and I have spoken about became angry and jealous over Miss Wellman working with me, and she grabbed Detective Wellman's camera purse that had captured everything from the beginning of the phenomenon to the end and stomped on it. We had it all. But to no avail. The camera was broken in too many pieces to be of any use. But I can return there and get the proof that the Legend of Hollow Pass is true. In fact, Miss Wellman and I were going there yesterday but were interrupted by Bishop Cullity."

As Matthew continued with his intriguing story, Bishop Cullity excused himself and left the room. He had heard enough of the tale Father Matthew was spewing and believed him to be on the verge of a nervous breakdown. He wanted Matthew to get some help before returning to the Church. So, he called the mental hospital and asked that

Father Matthew be taken there for a period of time until he was deemed fit to reenter society.

About ten minutes later, Bishop Cullity and three big and burly orderlies entered the room. Two of the orderlies came from behind and grabbed Matthew by surprise.

But Matthew was a pretty big guy and fought back, yelling, "Take your hands off of me. What are you doing? Stop!" He looked to the men at the table and pleaded with them to help him. "Please, help me. Why are you doing this to me?"

Finally, the third orderly was able to shoot him full of three hundred milligrams of Thorazine. Within seconds, Matthew was out like a light and as docile as a lamb. A stretcher was wheeled into the room and Matthew carried out on it and into their ambulance. They transported him directly to the mental hospital and placed him into a straightjacket just before placing him into a padded room and the same room that had housed Senator Strang's wife.

Over the next few days, the hospital staff was giving Matthew his daily doses of Thorazine and many psycho tropic drugs to keep their patient calm, drooling and docile.

Hampton and Wellman, however, were worried about Matthew because they hadn't seen nor heard from him in the last few days and believed something bad had happened to him.

The two detectives decided to make amends and end their feud to investigate Matthew's whereabouts, together.

***

Wellman had been with Matthew the morning Bishop Cullity showed up at Matthew's home for a meeting and she knew that Bishop Cullity was the last person to be seen with him.

Wellman's investigative instincts kicked in and she decided to visit with Bishop Cullity to interrogate him concerning the investigation of Matthew's disappearance. Pronto!

But before she went to the church to find Cullity she had one other thing to do; and that was to pick up Hampton to help in the interrogation and to be a witness to everything that was said and done because Wellman was not going to leave any stone unturned in her quest to find her friend. She was becoming enamored with Matthew. They had experienced things that not many people could experience. And those that had, have ended up missing. She was hoping that that hadn't happened to Matthew; that he hadn't returned to the Costume Shop alone, put on a costume and gone through that door, hoping to free the exiles in space. She prayed that hadn't happened. But just to be on the safe side, interrogating Cullity was a must. She was going to find out just what Cullity knew on the subject.

Wellman returned to the precinct and coaxed Hampton to join her in her quest to find Matthew. Hampton agreed and off they went, Wellman driving them directly to the church.

Wellman gave Hampton the low down. She was not to speak but only to watch and listen. Hampton agreed. Anything to find her *love*.

Soon after, the two ladies were in the church talking with Bishop Cullity. Wellman asked him the whereabouts of Father Matthew.

Cullity refused to answer her question. "It doesn't concern you," he snapped. "Father Matthew belongs to the Church. His life belongs to god, not loose women."

"Excuse me!" snapped the two women in unison.

"Leave Father Matthew alone!" yelled Cullity. "You two have caused him enough trouble. You're partly to blame for the trouble he's gotten himself into."

Wellman didn't want to hear it. "Where is Father Matthew?" she asked Cullity, her anger rising.

Cullity gave her a dirty look and remained silent.

"Okay, Bishop," warned Wellman. "I don't have time to play games. I came here asking for Father Matthew as Janet Wellman, his friend. Now I'm asking these questions as Detective Wellman. And if you refuse to answer my questions, I will arrest you on charges of hindering an investigation. I am not fooling around. And I don't care if you're good friends with Captain Bird, I want to know where Father Matthew is! And I want to know now! Where is he, Bishop Cullity?"

He remained silent for what seemed like hours but actually just seconds, then sang like a warbler. "He's at the insane asylum," he barked.

Wellman and Hampton were livid at hearing that statement. "Why is he there?" Wellman asked him. "Is he questioning one of the patients concerning his investigation of his father?"

Cullity shook his head, then answered in a soft voice, "No, now he's a patient there."

"He's what," the two women answered in unison.

"He's a patient at the asylum," repeated Cullity.

"You better be telling us the truth," Hampton demanded from Cullity.

"Miss, I'm a priest. I always tell the truth." After a few seconds, he said, smiling, "Unless I'm lying."

Wellman and Hampton looked at each other and decided to check and see if Cullity was telling the truth, by leaving the church and driving to the mental institution.

During their ride, they talked over a plan to get Matthew out of there, any way they could. Including, breaking him out if need be.

"I'll go in," Wellman explained, "and see what I can learn… and see if he is actually in there."

"What do we do if he's there?" Hampton asked her.

"We'll have to come up with a good plan. Either we sneak him out or we take him out in cuffs, as if we're arresting him for a crime."

"Yeah, but they won't release him unless the doctor signs off on it," Hampton surmised.

"Then we'll get a warrant and get him out with it and we'll bring one for the head doctor just in case he doesn't want to cooperate. We'll cart his butt off in cuffs too!"

The two investigators were anxious to see their friend… and hoped to see him coherent and in good shape. If not, heads would roll. Wellman and Hampton would see to that.

Neither had visited this particular mental institution. They had heard about the place, of holding the most violent and insane people with criminal tendencies, and others that were non-violent but mentally insufficient. Father Matthew fit none of those profiles.

Both women knew Father Matthew shouldn't be there. But Wellman knew that Matthew had to have said something at that morning meeting that someone took offense at. There was no other reason for Matthew to be a patient in an insane asylum. And they would find out who the guilty party was.

"You can bank on that!" Wellman said to Hampton.

Approaching the asylum, Wellman noticed a car following her, the same one that she had noticed following her to the church. She shook it off believing it to be paranoia, even though the car parked behind her car.

The two women were taken aback at the strange and gothic-looking building, the Willow trees weeping, the gargoyles looking over the ground for any enemies that lurk in the shadows were a bit much for their feminine minds. Hampton refused to wait in the car and went with Wellman.

Once inside, they looked around the prison-like surroundings, was aghast at the crumbling walls and dirty floors and were deafened by the painful cries and screams. It was… a madhouse!

But not a soul in sight… and nobody at the reception desk. They waited for nearly ten minutes before they were waited on.

"Hello, I'm Nurse Brachit. Can I help you?" she asked them.

"Yes," answered Wellman.

The two investigators showed her their identification.

"We're here to see one of your patients." Hampton told Brachit. "A Father Jack Matthew. Is he here?"

"Why? What did he do?" she asked, as she looked at her patient list.

Wellman told her that she just wanted to question him.

Brachit was hesitant. "I don't know if I can allow that."

Hampton tried a different approach. "Can we at least see him?" she asked Brachit.

"Why, what did he do? Rape some little boys?" Brachit, to say the least, was very inquisitive.

"Nurse, that's enough," snapped Hampton. "We need to see him. Now!"

The two investigators didn't take too kindly to Brachit's last comment. They knew Father Matthew as a virile heterosexual male who one day might take some lucky woman as his bride. At least one of these two detectives, if not both, were going to try their best to get Matthew to the Alter.

***

Nurse Brachit retrieved the keys and walked the two detectives up the four flights of stairs to the patient's room.

Each detective took their turns and looked through the tiny door window. Once two burly orderlies had showed up Brachit allowed the two women to enter the room. But not to question him, only to check up on his well-being.

When they saw Father Matthew in a straightjacket, stoned on drugs and drooling at the mouth, they were aghast at the treatment given to their friend. They wanted to take him out of that institution immediately.

"These conditions are horrendous," barked Hampton. "They're not fit for zoo animals let alone humans."

The two women tried to lift Matthew to his feet but it was very difficult to lift dead weight. He was just too drugged up and too heavy. Even if they could have gotten Matthew to his feet, they doubted seriously that the orderlies would have allowed them to leave with their patient. So, they sat him back on the mattress and promised Brachit that they'd return and take Father Matthew to another facility.

They retreated from the room, for now and waited near the receptionist desk talking over a plan. Just then, Brachit walked by and placed the keys in a drawer of the desk and then walked to the woman's restroom.

The two investigators needed to act fast. Wellman ran behind the counter and grabbed the keys from the drawer. They ran up four flights of stairs and to Matthew's room in record time. It took time to find the correct key from the key ring that fit the lock and just as they went to turn the key they heard voices nearby. So, they ran down the hall, away from the voices and hid into a closet until the danger had passed. But Wellman forgot to grab the key out of the lock. She was afraid the key and key ring wouldn't be there when they returned to the room. And she was right. It seemed when those voices walked by the room they saw the key in the door and took them.

Wellman and Hampton had to come up with a new idea to free their loved one out of that *madhouse*.

So, they left the asylum and headed for the precinct to get an arrest warrant to spring Matthew from his prison cell.

Wellman and Hampton, once inside the station went directly to Captain Bird and explained Father Matthew's situation to him.

"He needs your help!" begged Wellman.

Bird looked at the two women standing in front of his desk and went off on them. "I just want to let you two women know that I just got off the phone with Bishop Cullity and his people. What were you two thinking? Have you gals lost it? This infatuation you have with Father Matthew has got to stop."

"Sir," whined Hampton, "they've put him in an insane asylum. An insane asylum. Can you believe it?"

"And the place is disgusting and smells of death," interjected Wellman.

"I'm sorry, ladies. I can't help you. Bishop Cullity said that he's there to dry out. Father Matthew's a member of the Church. And we can't meddle in the church's affairs."

The women didn't want to hear it. "But sir," whined Hampton, "the conditions in that place are despicable. Father Matthew's been placed in a straightjacket, in a dirty and smelly room that you wouldn't keep a dog in. Can't we do something about that?"

"Call the Health department!" Bird replied, sarcastically. "Maybe they can do something for you. I can't. Now, please. Leave my office."

The girls let out a loud sigh before turning and walking out of the room. They went to Hampton's desk to plan their next move.

Wellman had an idea and ran it by Hampton. "What we need to get Jack out of the hospital is a warrant. That's the only thing that can override the doctor. And if he gets in our way, we'll arrest him too."

"What about the nurse?" Hampton asked her.

"We'll arrest her too if she interferes or assaults us."

"So, what judge are we going to get to sign the warrant?"

"I don't know, Carolyn. It might just be easier to forge one."

"What?" Hampton couldn't believe what she had just heard come out of Wellman's mouth.

Wellman actually wanted to break the law, to falsify a document and forge a judge's signature on the warrant.

Was Jack Matthew's well-being worth possibly losing their jobs and going to jail? That was the dilemma the two women faced.

They looked at each other and agreed with their plan of action. "Let's do it," they said in unison.

Hampton typed up the warrant and Wellman signed a judge's name to it. Now they were ready to face Brachit and company to free Matthew from his shackles.

***

The two women arrived at the asylum just ten minutes after leaving the precinct. They were anxious to confront the hospital personnel. If any of them were to get in the way, they would be taken out in handcuffs and thrown in jail, at least for the night. The two women wanted a chance to do to them, as they have done to their friend.

So, when Hampton and Wellman walked up to the nurses' station and sought out Nurse Brachit, they were in an aroused state of mind.

Brachit came out of her office and met with the two detectives. "What can I do for you, detectives?" she asked them.

Wellman took the warrant out of her jacket pocket and held it up. "We have a warrant for Father Matthew's arrest," she told Brachit. "We need to wheel him out of here, pronto!"

Brachit looked surprised and shook her head. "I'm sorry, I can't release Father Matthew unless the doctor releases him to you."

"Then you get him on the phone," demanded Hampton, "and tell him to release him. If not, we'll arrest him for interfering with police business. And the same goes for you, nursy!"

"That won't be necessary," Brachit replied, as she was taken aback by Hampton's abrupt rudeness. "Just let me get the keys."

She returned a few minutes later and walked them up to Matthew's room. She unlocked the door and allowed the two detectives to release Matthew from his bonds. But he was still in no shape to walk out of there. He needed to be wheeled out of there.

"Get a wheelchair," Hampton shouted to Brachit.

Brachit did as ordered and had an orderly get one from down the hall. The orderlies were going to help Matthew into it, but the two detectives would have none of it. They gently lifted him and placed him into it.

"Aren't you going to place him in handcuffs?" Brachit asked them.

The two gave Brachit a dirty look. "Does he look dangerous?" Wellman said, sarcastically.

"Alright, let's get him out of here," barked Hampton.

Matthew was then wheeled to the freight elevator, which took them to the first floor. Hampton left to get the car, while Wellman stayed with the patient.

After driving the car up to the front door, Hampton returned to help Wellman push Matthew to the vehicle. They struggled to get him into the passenger seat but after a few tries, they accomplished their task. Hampton strapped him into his seat, while Wellman ran over to the other side of the car and got behind the wheel. The second Hampton had jumped into the back seat and closed the door, Wellman peeled out of the driveway and headed away from that god-awful place.

"Where are we going to take him?" Hampton asked.

Wellman thought for a few seconds, then replied, "Good question! Let's take him back to his place. We'll clean him up and put him to bed. Then we can decide our next plan of action."

"But what if someone from the Church comes looking for him?"

"We'll just tell them that we're cleaning him up before carting him off to jail."

"I hope it works," said Hampton, crossing her fingers for good luck.

They did as Wellman suggested and went straight to Matthew's abode. But on the way, Wellman noticed that same car as before following her. She couldn't understand why they would be following her, but in that moment in time, just wasn't important. Her worries were focused on Father Matthew.

When Wellman pulled up in Matthew's driveway, they remembered that they had no wheelchair to put him in so they had to lug his dead weight out of the car, across the lawn, up three steps to the porch, and then had to drag him through the front door, which was left unlocked, and into his home.

They dragged him into the bathroom and placed him into the bathtub, took off the only clothes he had on: a dirty and urine-soaked hospital gown, and turned on the warm water.

After a minute or two in the water, Matthew finally stirred and opened his eyes for a second or two but then closed them, still in a drugged-out stupor.

The two women washed *every* part of his body, and afterwards, they lifted him out of the tub and then dried him off before dressing him in pajamas. When that task was finished they carried him into the bedroom and plopped him into bed, threw the blanket over him and sat on either side of him, watching his chest rise and fall. These two ladies were *gaga* over Father Matthew. Each wanted him for herself, but according to Matthew's words, he wanted neither; only god.

***

Early that morning, while the two women and Matthew were lying in the bed, Bishop Cullity was being told of

Matthew's arrest. Soon after, he made inquiries, but Father Matthew had not yet been interred in the city jail. To find out more, he decided to speak with Captain Bird about the arrest and his two detectives. But that would have to wait a few more hours. Bird was still at home sleeping.

By the time Bird had arrived for work, Matthew had awakened, and with a clear head for a change.

Once Matthew dressed, Hampton and Wellman made a good and healthy breakfast for their guy, but he was in no mood for food. He wanted only drink. When the women objected, Matthew ignored their wishes and poured and chugged two double shots of whiskey.

Wellman looked at her watch and noticed her and Hampton were late for work and mentioned it to Hampton.

"Carolyn, I have to call the Captain and tell him we won't be in today and that we're investigating leads on Senator Strang's disappearance."

Hampton nodded. "Sounds good to me," Hampton replied.

But when Wellman made her phone call, Captain Bird had already heard from Bishop Cullity and wasn't all that pleased with his two female detectives. He ordered both women to the precinct immediately.

"You two have a lot of explaining to do," he told her. Before hanging up, he added, "And bring along Father Matthew."

Wellman slowly hung up the phone, then told the others about the conversation with Captain Bird. They were none too happy about returning to the precinct. Matthew was adamant with his decision to forego the meeting with Captain Bird and the city jail. He had just escaped from one jail with the help of his two friends and wasn't about to visit the city jail, and maybe end up there, and he sure wasn't about to make a return trip to that nuthouse. So, Matthew had to make a quick and wise decision; one which would decide his fate.

"My superiors," Matthew told them, "don't believe a word I said concerning the Legend. They think I'm crazy. They're the ones that had me locked up."

"So, what are you going to do?" asked Wellman.

"Only one thing I can do. Go to the Vatican and ask the Pope for permission to fight the spirits of Hollow Pass."

"When are you going to do that?" asked Hampton.

"Right now. That is, if you'll give me a ride to the airport. I won't even pack. I'll go with the clothes I have on and my American Express card. I don't leave home without it."

All three laughed at that comment.

Matthew took a few more shots of whiskey before his two friends drove him to the airport.

"Are we ready," he asked them.

"Let's go," the two women said in unison.

CHAPTER 9

The two women refused to drop Matthew off at the airport and decided to see him off. They followed him as far as they could go within the security perimeters before saying their goodbyes with crying eyes. Matthew promised them he would ***keep in touch***.

Within an hour, he had purchased his ticket and was flying in the wild blue yonder, heading for Rome, Italy to see his old boss, the Pope for permission to fight the evil of Hollow Pass.

Matthew was sure, after listening to his story, the Pope would agree that it had to be done. He prayed constantly during the flight for that exact outcome, and to land safely.

Upon arriving, he hopped a taxi and went directly to the Vatican. He knew a meeting with the Pope at this time was out of the question. Matthew decided to contact his old mentor for exorcisms: Father Joseph Pine.

To say the least, Pine was more than surprised at seeing Matthew in Rome.

"I thought you went back to the States for rehab," Pine said, not really happy to see his student. He could smell liquor on Matthew's breath. "I guess you didn't finish rehab, hey?" The two walked into the living room and sat down on the couch.

Matthew apologized for drinking but had an excuse. "I hate flying, Joseph, so I had a few drinks on the plane to settle my nerves."

"Jack, you don't have to make excuses for yourself. You're a grown man. But I **am** curious. Why did you come back?"

"I need your help. I need an audience with the Pope."

"You what!" Pine's eyes bugged out at the thought.

"I need permission for an exorcism in my home town."

"But you're on suspension," Pine reminded him. "You should be in rehab."

"But, but…"

"I know. You only had a few drinks on the plane." He shook his head in disgust.

Pine could see that Matthew wasn't in great shape like he used to be. He also noticed that his hair had gotten grayer, and had quite a few more wrinkles on his face, like a smoker's face, but Matthew never picked up the habit.

"So, what is this about an exorcism?" Pine asked. "Male or female?"

Matthew scratched his head and answered, "It's… It's…"

"Yeah, go ahead, Jack. Spit it out!"

"It's neither male nor female. It's more like a place."

"What?" Pine was confused. "Exorcise a place? What kind of place?"

"The only way I can explain it... is that it's a spirit world within a spirit world."

Pine shook his head in bewilderment. "Are you serious? A spirit world within a spirit world? And you want to tell this to the Pope? He'd have you committed."

"I've already been there," Matthew mumbled to himself.

"I'm sorry." Pine couldn't hear his answer.

"Nothing. I was just talking to myself."

"Well before you do anything I take it you have no place to stay."

Matthew explained how he came to the Vatican directly from the airport.

Pine offered Matthew his guest bedroom. "We'll get you dried out so you can ask Cardinal Gerhard to be reinstated. He's the Perfect for the Congregation for the Doctrine. If anyone can get you reinstated, it's the Cardinal. You can't exorcise anyone if you're not a functioning priest."

Matthew was hesitant and didn't give Pine an answer.

"Father Matthew," warned Pine, "if you ever want to work for the Church again you better heed my advice."

Matthew again remained silent. He was fighting his inner demons, not wanting to give up that drink.

"Listen to me, Jack. I'm twice your age… and once your mentor. I can help you… if you trust me."

Finally, Matthew relented and took Pine up on his offer.

"Where is your luggage, Jack?"

"This is all I brought with me," he replied, pointing to his black suit. He didn't wear his collar. He wasn't allowed to be a practicing priest. He did it at times back in the States only for specific and compassionate reasons.

"We'll find clean clothes for you tomorrow. Right now, I want you to relax. Dinner will be ready shortly."

Pine was true to his word. The housekeeper rang the dinner bell soon after Pine uttered those words. However, Pine had said that he wanted Matthew to dry out but yet served red wine with the meal. Matthew was about to question him about it but Pine beat him to the punch.

"I know what you're thinking," Pine said to Matthew. "But this is only red wine. Not that whiskey that your heart so desired. That was your downfall. You couldn't drink in moderation. You drank so much so fast that you were drunk within fifteen minutes. Moderation, Jack. Moderation!"

Matthew picked at his meal, but drank three glasses of the red wine. Pine cautioned him about it.

"Jack, easy does it on the wine. Remember. Moderation."

Matthew made the excuse that he had the shakes from alcohol syndrome, which meant that the alcohol had evaporated from his bloodstream and it wanted more. So, that wine helped ease the pressure on his head and body.

After dinner, the housekeeper brought Matthew clean clothes, pajamas and a robe of past guests. Soon after, he retired for the night and fell asleep easily. But a few hours later, Matthew again had that same dream, of his body being bombarded by fireballs exploding from that same Joker's mouth, burning his body to a crisp and seeing the ashes form those same three words; *jump thru door*. He awakened twice during the night, each time, his clothes drenched with perspiration.

Over the next few days, Matthew's health seemed to be getting better. He had cut out his whiskey drinking replacing it with red wine, readying himself for his meeting with Cardinal Gerhard.

But on the fourth day of Matthew's visit, Pine received a distressing phone call from Bishop Cullity. Cullity had learned that Matthew, after being rescued from the nut house, had flown to Rome hoping to see the Pope. Cullity wanted that meeting postponed.

"Why?" asked Pine.

Cullity explained to him the indignities Matthew had brought upon the Church and himself.

"I, myself, caught Father Matthew in an incriminating position with two women," Cullity told Pine. "He was standing in his living room practically naked with two women kneeling on the floor in front of him. I broke up the scene just before foreplay began."

"I didn't know this," Pine replied, confused by the news.

"He was also drunk," added Cullity. "And when he was supposed to be rehabilitating. Matthew got so bad he was committed to the mental institution in our city to dry out and get his head on straight. Well, he escaped... and evidently, ended up in Rome. But that's not the worst of it. He also has delusions about some spirit world that is taking souls to another universe. Father Matthew, I believe has had a nervous breakdown."

"Are you speaking of that Legend?"

"Yes. Has he told you about it too?"

He told him he had.

"And you think this is normal?"

"I'm sorry, Bishop Cullity. But I am not one to judge."

"But Joseph, it is now our responsibility to help Father Matthew with his troubled life."

"So, what would you like me to do?"

"Nothing," Cullity replied. "I will fly to Rome and see to it that Father Matthew is put away until he is fit to be a priest again."

Pine asked Cullity the date he would be arriving in Rome.

"I have a few things yet to take care of, so I will be there within three or four days. Father Matthew needs our help, Father Pine."

The conversation ended on that note. Pine was very worried about Father Matthew and the trouble that awaited him when Bishop Cullity arrived.

Pine was in a quandary. He didn't know where his loyalty lie: with Bishop or Matthew. He pondered with his conscious and asked for guidance from *the hand above*.

The following morning, Father Pine received his answer. He would do as he had planned and hopefully, have Matthew reinstated to the Order of Melchisideck before Bishop Cullity arrived in Rome.

Pine didn't feel as Cullity about Matthew's delusions concerning the Legend of Hollow Pass. Pine himself was an experienced exorcist dealing with the super natural and its spirits and demons. Although, he had never experienced anything like Matthew had mentioned but he couldn't rule it out. He knew Father Jack Matthew was not a liar. A drunkard and sometimes, compassionate fool but a storyteller, he was not.

Pine also decided not to tell Matthew about the phone call from Cullity. He wanted nothing to deter the reinstatement of his young apprentice. Matthew was one of the most intelligent and educated priests among the Order and had many great things to accomplish, only if he could get his drinking under control. Pine was helping Matthew do just that. But now with Cullity's arrival and his threats of having Matthew institutionalized, time was short for Matthew's rehabilitation.

Hoping to beat Cullity to the punch, Pine would have to act fast and set the meeting with Cardinal Gerhard within the next two days. Once Matthew was reinstated, Bishop Cullity and his followers would have no say in the matter and his threats would fall on deaf ears.

Unbeknownst to Pine, Bishop Cullity had already spoken to Cardinal Gerhard concerning the Matthew situation. Now it was up to Gerhard to ponder Matthew's fate.

The Cardinal also knew that Father Jack Matthew was a rising star within the organization. He wanted to hear from the accused before making a final decision. Indiscretions were one thing, delusional thoughts and criminal acts were another. He had some long and hard thinking to do on the matter. And like, Father Pine, Cardinal Gerhard also asked *the man above* for guidance.

The very next day, the Cardinal got his answer. Father Pine telephoned and got the meeting he had hoped for. Matthew would get his chance to speak with Gerhard and convince him that his reinstatement was warranted.

"Jack," said Pine, "I'm only going to give you one piece of advice. Please, don't mention to Cardinal Gerhard about that Legend that you spoke of. Don't let anything stop you from being reinstated. And right now, even though you're sober, that ghost town of spirits might sound a little whacky to him. He's never seen nor been to an exorcism and is not an exorcist like you or I. So be careful what you talk about. We have enough work ahead of us as it is. And I can't do it alone."

Father Matthew smiled and told Father Pine not to worry.

Pine remembered one important thing that he hadn't told Matthew and decided to tell him now. "Oh, I forgot to tell you that I got a call from Bishop Cullity. He's coming to Rome to see that you're sent back to America to finish your visit at the hospital. It seems the Bishop and the board are making a big stink about your idea to battle with the spirits and demons of Hollow Pass. So your reinstatement is essential."

Matthew seemed to get the message and nervously awaited his meeting with the Cardinal the following morning.

When the time came Matthew was reeling for a shot of whiskey to help settle his nerves but did without, while Pine was watching that is. Matthew was able to get his hands on a pint and hid it in his suit coat pocket. He brought it with him to the meeting just in case he needed a little extra courage.

Father Pine walked with Matthew to the Cardinal's apartment within the Vatican. Pine expected to participate in the meeting with Matthew and the Cardinal but it was not to be. When they entered the residence of Cardinal Gerhard, an assistant showed them to two different rooms. Pine went into a waiting room, while Matthew was led to the room where the meeting was to be held.

Matthew waited for some time before Gerhard finally showed up. While he waited, he began to get nervous and remembered the pint of whiskey he had hidden in his jacket pocket. He quickly looked around the room, and saw that the coast was clear, then pulled the pint out of his pocket. He unscrewed the cap, put the bottle to his mouth and in two gulps completely consumed the liquid; and just as fast, returned the bottle to his jacket pocket.

He was smiling and feeling no pain by the time Cardinal Gerhard came into the room.

"Hello," said the Cardinal, as the two shook hands for the first time.

Unfortunately, for Matthew, Gerhard smelled the alcohol on Matthew's breath, but didn't let on, not at that time anyway.

"Now, let us go into the drawing room and have some tea and talk. I'm told you'd like to get reinstated."

"Yes, Cardinal Gerhard, I have been rehabilitated and am fit for a position here at the Vatican again. In fact, Father Pine is hoping that he and I can work together again. So am I. We make a great team."

"So, you are not drinking anymore?" Gerhard asked him, looking deep into his soul.

Matthew looked down at the floor and lied. "No, I haven't been drinking, other than maybe a glass of wine every now and then."

Gerhard just shook his head in disbelief. He smelled the alcohol on his breath. But he let it go. Matthew seemed to hold his liquor well. He gave him the benefit of the doubt and figured the smell came from a glass of wine Matthew may have drunk.

Gerhard slapped his legs. "Okay, you say you're rehabilitated but why were you just recently in the mental hospital, which I'm told you escaped and traveled here to Rome."

Matthew was at a loss for words. He realized then that the news of his exploits had crossed the Atlantic.

"And what about these women that you are seeing and having inappropriate relationships with. That is not good for a priest. Especially with your knowledge and education. Father Matthew, you must be discreet with these matters. I know some women can become infatuated with a priest. They see everlasting peace for themselves in the afterlife if they can bed a priest. I was told that you were caught nearly having sexual relations with two women. Is that true?"

Matthew couldn't speak. He had taken in too much at one time from Cardinal Gerhard to even think. But after the shock wore off, Matthew finally gave him an answer.

"No, it's not true. I spilled a drink on myself and they were helping me get out of my clothes." Just then, Matthew realized that story sure didn't sound convincing. Even he now thought that his explanation lacked credibility.

Cardinal Gerhard didn't speak and just listened. He let Matthew dig his grave even deeper.

Matthew tried his best to sway the ***court of appeals*** and continued to plead his case. "I know it sounds bad but it was really an innocent scene. I spilled hot coffee on myself, and Detective Janet Wellman was working on a case with me. She was sitting next to me when I spilled the coffee and helped me get out of my very hot and wet clothes. And just as I was getting out of them, another Detective walked into the house and just as she was walking into the living room, Bishop Cullity of my Diocese came into my house and unfortunately, saw what was happening and thought we were having a sexual rendezvous. Which was way out of line."

Gerhard interrupted Matthew's explanation. "I'm curious. What case were you working on with two detectives?"

"I don't really want to talk about it, Cardinal Gerhard."

"Yes, but I want you to. What case were you working on?"

Reluctantly, he spilled his guts. "I was investigating my father's disappearance. He went missing quite a few years ago. Detective Carolyn Hampton started the case with me; she was transferred to another case and Detective Janet Wellman came aboard. She was working another missing person case that involved a state Senator. And during our investigation we saw and heard some very strange things."

While Matthew was explaining his case to Gerhard hoping for reinstatement into the Order, another person was waiting in the wings hoping to see Matthew returned to the States and to the isolation room of the insane asylum to which he escaped from. And Matthew was very aware that this could be a possibility.

What Matthew, and Pine, for that matter, were unaware of, was that the person waiting in the wings was Bishop Cullity. He had already arrived in Rome and was also at the meeting, standing just twenty feet away hidden by a hallway wall and listening to every word said. But Matthew's words weren't important to him. Bishop Cullity had a surprise for Father Matthew. And it was by no means a *good* surprise. Bishop Cullity brought with him a Vatican nurse and security team, just to be on the safe side. Matthew was still strong as an ox and might need sedation.

"What strange things did you see," Gerhard asked Matthew, but already knew the answer.

Matthew continued with his explanation. "Sir, what I'm about to tell you, I've been warned not to talk about. It's a story back home that some call the Legend of Hollow Pass. I had the proof that the Legend actually existed. But the evidence was damaged to the point of no return. I can get that proof again if given the chance. And I can save the souls that are paying for their ancestors' mistakes."

"What are you talking about? Make sense!" barked Gerhard.

"Sir, the legend begins back around the end of the Civil War, when a town of newly immigrants massacred a whole village of Indians, men, women and children. But before all were killed it was said that the medicine men put an evil curse on them, which worked because the whole town was killed from the plague. And because those Indians weren't given an Indian burial so their souls could go to their god, they are taking the souls of the descendants so the Indian souls can finally reach Indian heaven. The thing of it is, the souls of the descendants are in a spirit world within a spirit world, in a type of black hole. I *and* Detective Wellman heard the cries of these people. Which means they are still alive. I believe I can fight the spirits and demons of this evil realm and release and return the innocent to their time in space. That's why I need to be reinstated. I don't want any more people disappearing and ending up as a missing person. This will continue for eternity unless it's stopped. And one of my professions is exorcism."

Cardinal Gerhard thought too many of Father Matthew's brain cells had been lost due to alcohol poisoning.

Cardinal Gerhard excused himself and left Matthew alone.

Matthew paced back and forth, wishing he had a little more whiskey in his bottle. His nerves were shot.

When Gerhard left the room, he motioned for Bishop Cullity to do his duty for the Church.

Matthew had his back turned when Cullity and crew snuck into the room. Just as Matthew turned to see who had crept up behind him, it was déjà vu' all over again. Two burly security guards grabbed an arm each and held him while the nurse gave him a sedative, which knocked him out in less than ten seconds.

Matthew was as docile as a newborn lamb. They placed him onto a stretcher and took him out the back way, bypassing anyone in the outer rooms.

They took Matthew away in an ambulance and went directly to Rome's mental facility where they dumped him off until other arrangements could be made.

But Matthew wasn't as unconscious as first thought. When the people that were responsible for Matthew's incarceration were away far across the room filling out paperwork, Matthew saw that it was his chance to escape. But when he tried to stand he was too groggy and weak. But he saw that just a few feet away, on a small counter lay a phone. He looked around to see that the coast was clear and then crawled the short distance to the phone.

Dialing Wellman's cell phone number, he prayed she could help him get out of this new *fix* he had found himself in. "Please pick up," Matthew mumbled to himself. "Please pick up."

She picked up on the second ring.

Matthew was able to tell her what had happened to him.

She promised to be on the first plane to Rome.

Matthew had enough energy to crawl back to the stretcher without anyone being the wiser. He would just have to wait it out for the cavalry to arrive.

***

While Matthew was lying on the stretcher, Pine was still unaware that Matthew had been taken away. It wasn't until a few hours after Matthew had been delivered to

Rome's mental hospital that Pine was finally told of the outcome of the meeting.

To say the least, Pine was none too happy. He needed Matthew reinstated. He had many cases of people that were possible candidates for exorcisms and needed Matthew to look over their profiles and evidence to verify their viability for Vatican sanction involving their exorcism. This was important to not only Pine, but to the Church. Fighting demons and spirits had been sanctioned by the Church for many centuries and had been hazardous duty for many a good priest. Pine didn't want to be another statistic in church history as another martyr biting the dust for fighting demons and spirits. Not without a fight, anyway.

Pine would fight for Matthew's release and reinstatement. If not granted, Pine decided he would retire and fight no more.

Wellman was also one who would fight for Matthew's release. And her fight started the minute she hung up the phone.

CHAPTER 10

Wellman was true to her word. She was at the airport within an hour and had taken a friend and colleague with her for an extra hand in breaking their friend, once again, out of a mental facility.

While Wellman and Hampton were on the plane flying to Rome, Matthew was being subjected to electric shock therapy, isolation, heavy sedatives, placed into a straightjacket and starved of food and drink.

Bishop Cullity was behind the assault on Matthew, hoping to knock some sense into him and rid him of his crazy ideas that had to do with the Legend of Hollow Pass.

The workers at the asylum were really putting the screws to Matthew, on behalf of Cullity and the Church.

Matthew was thrown into a padded room completely naked, only a straightjacket as clothing, laying on a dirty mattress on the floor and in a drugged stupor.

He rambled on, slurring the words: "The Legend. The Legend." Those were the only words that he had spoken, when he was semiconscious. Other times, he was literally completely incoherent due to the drugs given him.

As Matthew desperately tried staying alive, Wellman and Hampton had landed at the airport in Rome. Instead of taking a taxi to a hotel, they wanted to find Matthew and get him out of the *hell* that he was surely in. His own Church and the people that he trusted, turned on him and had him thrown in an insane asylum where he was being abused and used—again!

Wellman and Hampton feared the worst for their beloved friend and had the cab driver take them directly to the only mental institution in Rome, specifically used for derelict Catholic priests.

The two women had worked out a plan of escape for Matthew and hoped to put it to good use.

When they reached the facility, they were taken aback by the old and strange-looking building, very similar to the asylum in their hometown. But much older and with many, many more gargoyles overlooking the grounds warding off any spirits or demons that wanted to call the hospital "home."

When the two detectives finally entered the condemned-looking interior of the hospital, they were somewhat spooked by the wailing and screaming of many of its patients, but found the courage within themselves and walked directly to the nurse's counter in the middle of the floor. They produced their police identification and showed it to the nurse behind the counter.

The nurse looked at their badges and identification, then said in broken English, "American?"

The two detectives smiled and said in unison, "Yes."

The nurse held up her hand to stop the conversation, then yelled out to another nurse on the other side of the room, "Americans!"

That nurse walked over and joined the crowd at the counter. "You two Americans?" asked the young nurse in broken English.

"You understand and speak English very well," said Wellman.

"Why you here?" she asked them.

Hampton jumped into the conversation and told her they needed to see Father Jack Matthew. "He's an escapee from an American mental facility and we will be extraditing him back there. We were told that he came here sometime last night."

"You want him for...?"

"We need to look in on him..." interjected Wellman. "And we need the paperwork of his incarceration. We need it for our records. And make sure Matthew will be all set to go when the time comes."

The interpreter spoke to the head nurse in Italian, evidently telling her to get the paperwork, which she did and handed it to Wellman. The interpreter then directed them to Matthew's room, which took them nearly five minutes to find. He was in a desolate part of the hospital. It was like being in solitary in a prison ward. It was pathetic.

The door opened and the two lonely detectives saw their loved one in disarray and naked. "What are you people doing?" Wellman asked the interpreter in anger. "Get me a blanket to wrap around him. Then get me his clothes. I want him dressed when we take him out of here!"

"Are you taking him now?" the interpreter asked her.

Wellman shook her head. "No. We have to finish the paperwork first. We will be here early tomorrow morning to take him out of here. So, get him cleaned up and ready for shipment. We have to get him back to the States as soon as possible."

The meeting ended and they left the room, that is, all but one. Hampton stayed behind, not wanting to leave Matthew alone in that god-awful place.

"Come on, Carolyn," Wellman begged. "We need to get this paperwork done." She grabbed Hampton by the arm and pulled her from the room.

As they exited from the building, Hampton stopped Wellman and wanted an explanation. "Why didn't you take him out now? We could have been on a plane to the States within an hour or two."

"Carolyn, we have to make it look as though we are doing this legally. I don't want them to get suspicious. They know now that we are taking him out in the morning."

The two woman drove to their hotel and made more plans for Matthew's escape. They decided to hire an ambulance, driver, and attendant, who would dress up as a doctor. They knew that Matthew would not be in any shape to walk on his own. The two women went through that hassle once before. They wouldn't do it this time. They would carry Matthew out on a stretcher, take him to the airport, place him in a wheelchair and wheel him through security to the boarding gate. That was the plan anyway.

The rest of the day, they searched the city for an ambulance company that would help them in their quest. They went from place to place, but not one was interested in helping. Not even for a large sum of money. They were just about ready to give up and then decided to try one last company, which was in the seedy side of Rome, basically, in the sewers of Rome. The streets were full of shady looking men, all with guns sticking out of their waistbands.

The two detectives were sure not to show their badges in this side of town. They finally found the place they were looking for and asked the owner for help, and he agreed; for a large sum of money, he would give them everything they asked for.

Wellman promised to hand over the money in the morning and the owner agreed. The two women really didn't trust him because he too carried a gun in his waistband. But they had no other choice.

So everything was set for the morning. The two women barely got any sleep going over and over every step in their plan so there wouldn't be any mistakes. They even went to a print shop and had an authentic extradition document printed up to show anyone who asked for it.

Wellman and Hampton were anxious to get the ball rolling.

***

The following morning, the two detectives took a cab to the ambulance company. The owner came through and had everything ready for the breakout; the ambulance with stretcher, driver dressed in "whites" and the attendant dressed as a doctor, stethoscope included. The money was paid and the two women then followed the ambulance to the asylum.

The group arrived at exactly six am. The ambulance pulled up to the entrance, the driver and doctor got out and grabbed the stretcher from the rear of the ambulance, then followed the two women into the building.

Waving the extradition paper in the air for all to see, Wellman went directly to the nurses' counter to make her presence known, while Hampton and the others followed.

Wellman sought out the interpreter for her help in rescuing Father Matthew, hoping no questions would be asked in the freeing of their loved one.

The interpreter was found and the detectives were taken to Matthew's room. He wore only a hospital gown but his clothes and passport were in a small duffle bag.

Matthew was heavily medicated and barely coherent. He had no strength in his legs to stand and both Hampton and Wellman noticed that Father Matthew had gotten older overnight. His hair even grayer than before and his face had become weathered and wrinkled. He looked sixty now, not his actual age of thirty-two.

Hampton had noticed the same change in Wellman but out of respect for her friend never mentioned it. But that wasn't important at this particular time. What was of utmost importance was to get Matthew out of the asylum and into the ambulance, then to the airport.

The plan was working well. No one questioned the detectives' motive. Facing an Extradition Order was a very good reason to hand over a patient. But being too confident nearly cost them their patient.

As Wellman and company were exiting the building, Bishop Cullity and his entourage were entering the building. Their eyes met but recognition did not take place. Not at that particular time. It was sometime later that both Wellman and Cullity realized who the other was.

Cullity remembered the second he saw that Father Matthew had been snatched from his room by two women. That's when it dawned on him. The woman at the door was the same woman that he had seen in Matthew's living room that day he caught Matthew nearly naked and her kneeling in front of him. Now he had to find Matthew but had no idea where the two women had taken him. Now, he would have to do some investigating on his own.

Cullity and company were angry and disgusted with the hospital workers lack of responsibility for their actions and promised to get them all fired. He then returned to Cardinal Gerhard's residence to give him the news.

Matthew on the other hand, was being dressed in the back of the ambulance by the two women who were madly in love with him or at the very least, very infatuated with him. He was slowly coming to but was still very groggy.

They reached the airport without a hitch. Matthew was placed into a wheelchair and wheeled into the airport.

After buying tickets and checking in, Matthew was wheeled through security and to the departing gate. By this time, Matthew was coherent enough to speak.

"Janet," Matthew whispered. "I want you to call Father Pine at the Vatican. Tell him that I'm alright and am returning home."

He gave her the phone number and she did as asked.

Pine was happy to hear from her. "Don't go anywhere," he pleaded. "I need to speak with Father Matthew. It's a matter of life and death."

Wellman was hesitant to tell him there whereabouts, but at Matthew's urging, she did.

"I'll be there in less than twenty minutes," Pine told her. "Please wait for me. I have some good news for Father Matthew."

Pine was true to his word. He arrived at the airport in fifteen minutes. After getting permission to bypass security to get to the departing gate where Matthew and company were awaiting their flight to the States, he used all his persuasive powers to talk Matthew into staying in Rome.

"Jack, come back," Pine begged. "I've got Cardinal Gerhard's promise that you will be reinstated. Maybe even today!"

"Why, now, all of a sudden?" Matthew asked him.

"He's going back home with us," Hampton barked.

"I'm sorry, Miss. But Father Matthew is needed here," said Pine.

"Why?" Matthew asked him.

Pine explained to him how Pope Francis's niece had been acting strangely and doing some crazy things and possibly needed to be exorcised. "And your expertise is needed, Jack." He continued. "There are also twelve candidates that could possibly qualify for an exorcism but you must vet each one and decide if they truly need it or not. I'm sure some of these people will need our help to rid their souls of the spirits and demons within. Right now that's far more important than ridding some ghost town of its demons. You have plenty of time for that. But the Pope needs your help now!"

"I don't know," replied Matthew. "How do I know I won't get thrown back into that nut house again?"

"Trust me, Jack. I promise you. The Pope has your back!"

"Don't trust them, Jack!" Hampton said, angrily. "You trusted them once in America, and look what they did to you. You trusted them in Rome and they did the same thing to you. Let's go back home."

"Jack," interjected Wellman. "We still have work to do concerning Hollow Pass. And you and I are the ones that can bring those people home."

But Matthew knew better. "But Janet, I have to be reinstated in the Order before I can use my priestly vows. I can't fight any demons without that."

"So, the best thing for you," Pine said to Matthew, "is to come back to the Vatican. Cardinal Gerhard promised your reinstatement just as soon as he can get the Commission together. Fight our demons first, before fighting those of Hollow Pass. I have faith in you, Jack. Now have faith in me. It wasn't me that had you thrown in that institution, it was Bishop Cullity and his board members that were responsible. I am on your side. Now be on mine."

The two women wanted him to fly back to America with them. Matthew was in a dilemma. He was torn between fear and love. Half of him wanted to flee back to his home town, the other half still wanted to adhere to the vows he had taken for the priesthood.

Matthew decided to choose love. He gave his two saviors the bad news. "I'm sorry, ladies. My heart belongs to the Church."

The women didn't want to hear it. They just flew all the way from America and rescued him from a hell hole and now he wants to push them aside and possibly get thrown into that hell hole again.

Matthew heard them loud and clear and looked at Pine for reassurance. "I'm trusting you with my life, Joseph. I pray you're not lying to me."

"Well, if you're staying, I'm staying," remarked Hampton.

"That goes for me too," added Wellman.

Pine intervened. "Please, ladies! Father Matthew has had enough surprises for one day. Let him get back to the job he was meant for. Now, if you'll excuse us."

Pine began pushing Matthew in his wheelchair. Matthew was still too weak to stand, let alone walk a mile through the airport before reaching the outdoors. The two women tried to stop Pine from taking their loved one from them so Matthew had to scold them like children.

"Janet! Carolyn! Stop it! You're acting like school kids, fighting over me. I'm a priest! Yes, I'm your friend, but that's as far as it goes. I've told you two over and over again that I'm a ***man of the cloth***. But you don't hear a word I say. Had I been a called for a different purpose in life, just a regular guy, I might have sexual feelings towards you. But I've been called by ***god***... to do his work, to make sacrifices. And this is ***my*** choice. I appreciate all you've done for me. But now it's time to part ways. You two beautiful ladies have jobs to go back to. I suggest you get back to them before they fire you. Thank you for everything."

Just at that moment, the passengers began boarding the plane for America. Now the two women were in a dilemma. Should they go or should they stay? That was the very question they wrestled with. They looked at Matthew. They looked at each other. They were still undecided.

At that point, Pine began wheeling Matthew away again from the departing gate.

The two women picked love too and decided to stay by Matthew's side until he was reinstated. They would make sure that if he ended up in that insane asylum again, they would be ready to do whatever it took to break him out of the place.

Matthew gave up trying to talk sense into them, to return to America and their jobs.

The women didn't care. They would forego their jobs and their lives for the love of their dear friend. But they didn't have to stick by him for much longer.

Pine was true to his word. Three days after the airport incident, Cardinal Gerhard and the commission reinstated Father Matthew to his old position.

"We will place you on probation," Gerhard told Matthew. "If you do well and don't abuse your power or body, then, after one year, I will let you return to your hometown and then you can go fight your so-called spirits and demons with the Church's blessing in that place you called…"

"Hollow Pass!" answered Matthew with a smile.

Afterwards, Father Matthew was seen by Pope Francis for a meeting concerning his niece. The Pope wanted Matthew to look in on his niece paying special attention to her odd behavior and schizophrenic mind. He believed she either had a split personality or was actually possessed. Father Matthew was going to interview her and decide her best type of treatment.

Matthew was to assist Father Pine in any and all exorcisms if warranted. They had Pope Francis's blessing. They were to keep Cardinal Gerhard abreast of any news good or bad. He in turn would relay the message to "your holiness" if the news concerned him.

Pine and Matthew got right to work. They had twelve cases to investigate and decide the best course of action.

CHAPTER 11

Wellman and Hampton finally returned to America, saddened by the loss of their dear friend. They left not knowing if they'd ever see or hear from Father Matthew again. But as soon as they arrived back in their hometown, they both wrote him every day. Hampton wrote to him about one day being together forever. Wellman on the other hand, wrote that she was going to continue gathering evidence to prove that the Legend of Hollow Pass wasn't just a legend but really existed, just in a different realm, a different dimension. Even though she was ordered not to get involved in that nonsense, she refused to listen to her superiors and suddenly, nearly a year later, she left the precinct and never returned, never to be heard from again. She suddenly disappeared and became a missing person's investigation with Hampton at the helm.

***

Matthew worked hard and long and participated in three exorcisms. He and his co-worker, Father Pine, had seen and interviewed twelve people, including the Pope's niece. It was decided that three were qualified for an exorcism. The Pope's niece was diagnosed by Matthew as having multi-personalities—at least three if not more as time passes. She was put in touch with an excellent psycho therapist and psychiatrist. Over time, with the right medication and therapy, she could hopefully conquer her inner demons.

The first of the three exorcisms was in Venice; a female, aged thirty and single. PET scans of the brain showed signs of activity that had never been seen before. They saw constant color changes within many different parts of the brain when the demon took over the patient's body. Parts of the brain that hadn't been used since Neanderthal days.

The two exorcists recorded and filmed their work for three days before ending their exorcism. This one had gotten out of hand. The exorcism was too much for this beautiful woman. She died of a heart attack, which they believed was due to fright. She was frightened to death by the demon within. Laying on the cross burned her skin; the holy water that landed on her skin brought puss boils all over her body; her talking in tongues and in two or more voices at once. Some people trained in song can sing two different voices at once. But not three, like the female patient had done.

The two priests did their best, but their best just wasn't good enough. The worst thing of all was that they didn't know if the demon had died with her or if it escaped and found another innocent person to torment.

The second exorcism was in Naples; a forty-six year old male had been tormented for years by inner voices that had completely taken over his body and mind. To get control of the demons, the two priests tried something different. They decided drops of holy water on the body wasn't enough to draw the demons away from the host's body. So, they filled a plastic gallon tank and sprayer with holy water and sprayed not only the naked body of the patient but also soaked the pillows and sheets in the special liquid.

While Matthew sprayed, Pine had placed a small cross on each side of the patient's head until the smell of burning hair and skin filled the room. The demons screamed in painful cries. Matthew sprayed even more holy water on the patient's body until the screams of torment filled the room.

Pine chanted verses from the Bible while Matthew continued spraying the bed and body. The demons tormented cries became louder and louder, making the body shake uncontrollably. Matthew sprayed the patient with more holy water. Pine, doing his thing with the crosses.

The shrill cries from the demons shook the windows, a putrid smell filled the room, and intense heat suddenly filled the air, cutting off the breath of the two priests.

Matthew sprayed the last of his holy water onto the patient, until the patient stopped shaking and inhaled a deep breath of air, as if he had been reborn. The cries of the demons suddenly stopped and the smell and heat dissipated.

The priests had won their battle with the patient's inner demons, this time. They prayed that they wouldn't return any time soon. Their prayers were answered because three months later, both Pine and Matthew interviewed their male patient once again, then had a PET scan done at the local hospital and it showed none of the symptoms as before. His life had improved drastically and he was happy and working once again.

The priests' job was done for this subject. Now they were off to Torento, for exorcism number three, that of a young boy, age twelve and unresponsive. Only when the priests came upon the boy did the demon lash out at them. The boy had no control of his body. Just as Matthew had experienced at Hollow Pass Mountain.

Matthew was confident that this demon would die of a painful death and never torment anyone anymore. Again, he had filled the gallon tank with holy water and soaked the boy and bed with it. The demon screaming curse words and painful cries, making the boy thrash about in his bed. Pine using the crosses once again, placing them in strategic places on the boy's head and body.

They recorded and filmed their work for more than four days around the clock. It was tiring, to say the least. The exorcisms were taking their toll on their minds and bodies, especially Matthew's, for he kept looking older, his face adding wrinkles daily and his hair nearly white, and so young yet. He looked twice his age.

Pine chalked it up to Matthew's heavy drinking, which he could never get under control; he just never got out of control, is what had saved him so far.

The two never gave up their quest to rid the boy of his powerful demon. Matthew continued spraying the holy water, while Pine chanted Bible verses, basically doing the same things as they had at their last exorcism.

It had taken four days of fearless fighting with the evil entity before it had given up and dispersed from the boy's body.

That was two wins in a row for the two exorcists. Now it was time to return to the Vatican where they could rewind and rest up for their next adventure.

Matthew's next adventure, however, would take place in his hometown in America. His year of probation was nearly complete. Just a few more days in Rome and then his flight home.

Halloween was just around the corner, which was perfect timing for his fight at Hollow Pass. However, he would have to do it on his own this time. Wellman could no longer help him in his endeavor. He may end up, though, helping her return to the real world, if, in fact, she had been taken by the spirits and demons of Hollow Pass.

***

The first thing Matthew did after arriving home was to relax and get drunk in his living room without anyone around to bother him. Or so he thought. A knock on the door brought reality back to his attention. Answering it, he was surprised to see the back-stabbing Bishop Cullity standing in front of him.

Cullity looked at the bottle of whiskey in Matthew's hand.

Matthew really didn't give a damn. "Yes, Bishop Cullity," he said, slurring his words. "What do you want? To lock me up in that nut house again?"

"I see you're up to no good again, Jack."

"Hey, I just got back from Rome. I'm enjoying myself. Now if you'll excuse me."

As Matthew shut the door, Cullity threatened him. "You are now part of my Diocese. Don't get out of line or you will answer to me. And if I ask for your suspension and get it, I'll make sure you never wear the robes again." He turned and stormed off.

Matthew slammed the door and returned to his living room to drink the night away, hopefully without any more interruptions. He prayed for no more interruptions. Evidently, god didn't hear him.

Soon after, none other than Carolyn Hampton came to say hello.

Matthew invited her in, not seeing her for nearly a year. They talked about the disappearance of their friend and caught up on recent issues. They celebrated their friendship with lots of booze.

Hampton began flirting with Matthew and the more they drank, the flirting became more rampant, until they ended up in bed and consummated their friendship.

"That was wonderful," remarked Hampton, just after the two had awakened.

"We should have done it long ago," answered Matthew.

Matthew was disgruntled and dismayed with his Diocese and Bishop Cullity because Cullity had it in for him. Matthew wasn't in Rome any longer and had to conform to Cullity's views or hang it up. So, Matthew decided to hang it up. But not before he had completed his task, and that was to defeat the demons of Hollow Pass and rescue the victims taken for their ancestors' mistakes.

"Why don't we take our relationship to the next level?" Hampton asked her lover.

"And what level is that?"

She mentioned the "M" word. "Marriage!"

Matthew was taken aback by the suggestion, but only for a few seconds. After thinking it over, he gave an answer that even surprised Hampton.

"I'll tell you what! I've got to take care of this business with Hollow Pass. If I return, I'll leave the Church and we'll get married. How does that sound to you, Carolyn?"

Hampton was too happy to reply, instead grabbing her lover and hugging him to death. "I love you, Jack," Hampton said, giving him kisses all over his face.

"Okay, okay. Stop!" He pushed her away and got up to get dressed, as did Hampton.

After dressing, the two lovebirds had breakfast at the kitchen table. Soon after, Hampton poured her lover a shot of whiskey, something she knew he would need and enjoy. Matthew chugged them down as fast as she poured. She stopped pouring at four.

Matthew told Hampton that he had to visit Captain Bird before his trip to Hollow Pass. "I have to ask him about Janet."

"Forget about her," Hampton answered, jealous over the fact that her soon-to-be husband still had thoughts about her.

Matthew shook his hand. "I can't. I'm the reason she's missing. She wrote me and mentioned that she was going to investigate Hollow Pass herself. I believe that the demons have her and it's my fault."

Hampton tried soothing Matthew's feelings. "Don't fret over it, baby. She's a big girl... and knew what she was doing. Remember, she was a Missing Person's detective and her job was to investigate people that were deemed **missing**. No matter where the investigation may take them. Evidently, her investigation led her to Hollow Pass and it got the best of her. Leave it alone."

Matthew refused to listen to his new-found love. "I'll see you at the precinct," Matthew told her, as they walked out the door and went to their separate vehicles.

They both arrived at the precinct together and entered the building holding hands, even though Matthew had his collar on showing he was a priest.

Hampton went directly to her desk, while Matthew walked into Captain Bird's office. As he entered the room he noticed a man in his forties sitting in a chair speaking to Bird. Their conversation ended when Matthew was noticed.

"Father Matthew," Bird said, standing to shake his hand, "how are you doing? Long time no see!" He then introduced the man sitting. "And this is a man you should meet. He was a good friend of you father's. Meet Bobby Legend. He's a news reporter and journalist."

The two shook hands and took their seats.

"Glad to meet you, Father," said Legend.

Matthew nodded.

"Yeah," continued Legend, "I don't know if you know this but your father and I had a special interest in the Legend of Hollow Pass."

"Oh, is that right," remarked Matthew.

Legend nodded. "Yes, he gave me Detective Brad Zoolu's journal about his investigation of his partner at the time, a Detective Waters. That journal broke the story of Hollow Pass wide open. It got people talking again. That's why I'm here. Someone broke into my house and stole it and other things your father had given me. I've come here to ask Captain Bird for his help in getting those things back."

Matthew and Legend both looked to Bird for an answer.

Bird told Legend he would do what he could. "But it's not high on my agenda for crimes to solve. We've got another couple of days before Halloween and already we've had eight people come up missing. But the Legend has nothing to do with it!"

"Whatever you say, Captain," the two said in unison, looking at each other, then laughing.

Matthew turned to Legend and said, "You know, Mr. Legend, I'm investigating my father's disappearance and it involves the Legend of Hollow Pass. Captain Bird, I'm sure you know doesn't believe in superstitious nonsense. Especially, when it comes to the Legend. But I'm about to prove him wrong, and if I'm right, I should have a good story for you, Mr. Legend."

"Okay, okay," Bird said, abruptly interrupting the conversation. "Take that kind of talk out in the hallway. I don't want to hear that crap in my office. So, if you two are finished, you can leave any time."

Bird, to put it mildly, wasn't too happy with the way the conversation was going and put an end to it.

Matthew, however, wasn't finished. "Oh, I actually came in here to talk about the Wellman investigation," he told Bird. "Is there anything new?"

Bird shook his head. "Ask Hampton, it's her investigation."

Matthew told Bird he didn't need to speak with her. "Wellman, just may return to work if I'm right about my theory."

Bird had no idea what Matthew was talking about. "Father, I think you're losing it," he told him as Matthew and Legend walked out of the room.

Matthew turned and walked to Hampton's desk to say his goodbye, and gave her a long, passionate kiss, which her peers were shocked to see a priest kissing a woman so passionately. "See you soon, good-looking."

Matthew left his woman in tears as he hurried out of the building hoping to catch up with Legend. He had a few more questions for him.

Matthew caught up with him just as he was getting into his car. As he slid behind the wheel, Matthew asked him about Hollow Pass. "If you have a minute, I'd like to speak with you about the Legend."

"What would you like to know?"

He was asked if he liked hoagies.

Legend said he did.

"Follow me to Gabriele's Hoagie Shop. They serve great breakfast hoagies and alcoholic drinks."

Matthew hopped into his car and then sped away, heading for Gabriele's as Legend followed.

The two ate their breakfast hoagies and while digesting their meals had a few shots of whiskey to wash it all down.

This seemed to limber up their mouths and they spoke freely about their knowledge of the Legend.

Legend asked Matthew about his knowledge on the subject.

Matthew pulled no punches and let it all hang out. "I know a lot... because I am a descendant of those murderous killers, as was my father, Detective Zoolu,

Waters, Senator Strang and many, many hundreds of others. And I am going to try to rescue them."

Matthew looked Legend directly in the eyes to see his reaction to his words. He didn't know whether Legend believed him or not. But was somewhat surprised by Legend's response.

"You better get it done now," Legend said, mysteriously. "The window is closing. By my calculations the number of descendants that have been taken is nearing the number of Indians killed. Once that number is reached, I believe the window will close and Hollow Pass will be no more. It'll all be like a dream."

Matthew agreed. "You're right. I have to act now and hope and pray that I can defeat the spirits and demons that are taking our people. Well, Bobby, pray for me and wish me luck. I'll need it."

Bobby Legend laughed and pointed to Matthew's collar. "Father, I don't think you need my prayers. You talk to a much higher entity than me."

Matthew nodded with a smile.

The two shook hands and went their separate ways. Before leaving though, Legend asked a favor of Matthew.

"Father Matthew, if you make it, contact me would you please. I'd love to do the story."

Matthew agreed. "If I come back alive, you'll know my plan worked. If I don't, I hope you find somebody to save me. But either way, I'm sure you can find a story out of all this."

With that said, the two Legend hunters drove out of the parking lot in two different directions. Legend heading to god only knows and Matthew heading straight home to pack his car with the different objects needed to fight the demons. He wasted no time. He packed a full plastic gallon canister and sprayer with holy water, two large crosses, two Bibles, an extra collar, and last but not least, a full bottle of whiskey for a little extra courage for fighting. Then he was off to the races heading for Hollow Pass Mountain.

Two hours later, wap, zap, the explosion and he and his vehicle were climbing Mount Pass. He actually missed the sensation of being frozen in his car, not being able to move a muscle, while Mother Nature tried her hardest to kill him, spewing lightning, softball sized hail, hurricane winds that actually lifted the vehicle off the ground, pushing it towards the other side until it finally came to a stop at the start of the valley.

Matthew looked around to see if anything had changed. It hadn't. While he took it all in, he pulled the whiskey bottle from under his seat, opened it and began chugging its contents until there was no more. He had the courage now. Nothing was going to stop him in his fight to the finish. He put the car in gear, stepped on the accelerator and continued towards the ghost town that housed the Costume Shop. He was pretty sure it was still there, as a stopover for unsuspecting victims so the demons could fill their coffers.

He slowly crept upon the shop and noticed no other vehicles around. He would be the only customer in the place. He wondered if Joker was still behind the counter.

He grabbed the canister of holy water, placed the two crosses into his jacket pocket along with his extra collar and climbed the stairs to the shop. Before entering he placed the canister on the porch within reach of the open door. He didn't want to scare anyone or anybody at this point in time. His plan would take time to pull off.

Matthew slowly opened the door and peeked his head in. He saw no danger so he continued inside until the little man's and Matthew's eyes met.

"Can I help you, Father?" asked Joker.

"Do you remember me, Joker?" He was the same man Matthew remembered.

The little man behind the counter peered ever so intently at Matthew's face before slightly recognizing him.

"Yes," he said, "I do believe I remember you. You were here about this time last year. But you look so different now. Excuse me for saying this, Father, but it looks as though you've aged thirty years in just one. Is everything alright?"

"Yeah, everything's fine. I'm just here to rent a costume for a Halloween Ball."

Joker remembered a woman that came with Matthew.

"Where is the lady that came with you last year?"

"Oh, she's around here somewhere," Matthew remarked sarcastically. "I hope to see her in a little while."

"Is she going to the Halloween Ball with you? We have some great costumes I'm sure she'd like."

He nodded and smiled. "Oh, if you'll excuse me for a second I have to get my water I left in the car."

Matthew stepped outside for a minute and retrieved the water container then stepped inside again.

"What's that for?" Joker asked, not realizing that it was holy water.

"Oh, it's just in case the car breaks down out in the boonies and I have to walk in the hot sun. I drink a lot of water anyway. I always keep a gallon with me at all times in my old age."

"Ah, huh," mumbled Joker.

"Well, I'm looking for a costume similar to my own, but maybe with a little finer cut. You know, one that was maybe worn by a Bishop or Archbishop. Or maybe even a costume of a Cardinal. But then again, I don't look good in red. What have you got?"

"Look around. I'm sure you'll find something you like."

Matthew did just that and found what he had been looking for. Catholic robes fit for a king. He grabbed the costume and went into the dungy and dirty changing room.

A few minutes later, he came out to show Joker his new threads. "How do I look," Matthew asked him.

"Now all you need is a big cathedral to give your sermon."

Time was getting near when Matthew would put the rest of his plan in motion. Putting on the costume was part one of the plan. Part two was to spray Joker with the holy water to see what would happen. If Matthew's theory was correct, Joker should either melt or disappear like his counterpart had a year before.

Matthew picked up the container of holy water hooked the spray nozzle to it and sprayed the little man with a burst of holy water that settled upon Joker. The second it did, Joker burst into nothingness. He just disappeared. His clothes lay on the floor.

Matthew was overjoyed. So far, so good. Now the next step. He opened the door. But before he *jumped thru door*, he sprayed a cloudy mist of holy water outside, in the air and all around. The second he did this he heard ear piercing screams throughout the area in which he sprayed. Now Matthew sprayed more than ever. He put on his collar and then with container in hand, he *jumped thru door*. He was anxious and fearful on what he would confront on the other side.

As he jumped, he sprayed for all he was worth. An explosion of white light ensued and Matthew found himself in a black hole, a vortex. He was in a spirit world within a spirit world. The demons and spirits came after him, some flying in the air, some running, some jumping like animals. They came in all sizes and forms: werewolves, vampires, devils, anything and everything that looked hideous to one's normal self. But when they came in range of Matthew's special liquid, they imploded, or exploded, others evaporated into thin air. None could get in reach of him as long as he sprayed them with his holy water. But they were coming at him faster than he could spray.

And while fighting these demons and spirits, he could also hear the screams of the victims that were held in a vortex of their own. He didn't know yet how he would free them from their torment. But first things first. He had to wipe out any threat from these devilish entities before he could try to free the victims.

Those devilish entities continued to push forward, only to disappear into nothingness like the others. Suddenly, the demons and spirits were no longer a threat. In fact, they were no longer anywhere around. Only the voices of the victims could be heard.

Matthew had very little holy water left in the container. So, he took the two crosses out of his waistband, placed them into his left hand and held them into the air while chanting verses from the Bible and spraying what little bit of special liquid he had left. Suddenly, a bright white light came out of the center of total blackness, releasing its prisoners to freedom. One after another, flew away from that black hole and into the realm in which they came. Or so Matthew believed. And he was right, to an extent. They arrived from where they came alright, some landing in their homes, others on the streets or in their cars. But something happened in flight. They came back alive, but deformed, mutilated and some in pieces. None came back healthy and whole.

As Matthew was freeing the last of the victims, he felt faint and began to pass out from exhaustion. As he was falling he heard a loud voice come from the sky above.

"Doctor, Doctor," yelled a nurse, "he's coming around."

Another nurse shouted, "Oh my god, after six years he's out of his coma. Doctor, ask him some questions. See if he can speak."

"Mr. Matthew. Father Matthew, can you hear me. I'm Doctor Rhodes and I've been treating you since your accident."

Matthew looked around at his surroundings and noticed something very strange. It seemed as though he was laying on a cot in a large tent. There were no medical monitors or anything dealing with technology. He saw an old hack saw and bloody needles laying on a dirty dusty table. No televisions, no radios. Nothing.

"Where am I?" Matthew asked the doctor.

"You're at Hollow Pass hospital."

"Hollow Pass hospital? Where is that?"

"Where?" The doctor seemed confused by his questions. But then realized the patient had been in a coma for six years. He wasn't thinking straight yet. "Why you're in the Hollow Pass Army medical tent. You are the only surviving member of your town. You're one lucky man, Father."

Matthew was really confused now. He asked the doctor the year. "What year is this?"

"The year? Why it's eighteen sixty-six," the doctor told him.

Matthew became ill. His face went white, his body shook violently before he passed out. Suddenly, a loud ringing was heard, then buzzing and bells began clanging. A loud voice was heard.

"Mr. Legend. Mr. Legend, are you alright?" said a nurse.

"Boy," he whispered, "I had the weirdest dream."

He tried to sit up.

"Easy does it, Mr. Legend. You've been in a coma for many a year."

He looked around and saw that he was back in his time zone but didn't exactly know where. "Where am I?"

"You're in Hollow Pass hospital."

"What year is it?"

"It's two thousand and sixteen."

"Wow, I've been away for more than six years."

The nurse nodded while checking his vitals. Then the doctor came in the room to check on the patient.

"How are you doing, Mr. Legend?" asked the doctor.

"I dreamt that I was investigating the Legend of Hollow Pass and all my friends were disappearing from the real world to a spirit world. And I had to save them. Whew! It was one crazy dream."

"Boy," remarked the nurse, "you can say that again. What is the Legend of Hollow Pass? I've never heard of that before."

"I really can't remember too clearly. I think it was about something that happened just after the Civil War not too far from here. About how all the townsfolk from this one town massacred a whole village of Indians, men, women and children. Not one was spared. But before the Indians died, some of the medicine men put a curse on the townsfolk and I guess a few years later, all the people involved in the killings died from the plague. In my dream, only one survived. A priest. Father Jack Matthew. That's all I can remember."

"Well, don't worry yourself about it," said the doctor. "We've contacted your girlfriend and told her you have come out of your coma. She should be here very shortly."

"My girlfriend? Who is that?"

"Carolyn Hampton," the doctor reminded him. "Don't you remember?"

"Wow, she was in my dream too. This is weird."

"Well, if your vitals remain strong over the next day or so, we'll be able to release you and you can go home."

***

That evening Hampton came by to see her loved one. But Legend was distant. He couldn't remember having a girlfriend. He couldn't remember much of anything except that crazy dream.

Hampton was put off by her boyfriend, but she understood that he had been ill and it would take time for Legend to get back into the swing of things. So, she wasn't that worried about his memory. He would get stronger by the day and she would see to it that his every need was fulfilled.

Three days later, Legend was released from the hospital. He waited for Hampton to pick him up but she didn't show so he had the nurse wheel him to the front door in a wheelchair, then he would take a cab to his residence.

As Legend exited the doors of the hospital, a sudden dusty gust of wind came up and sand blew into his eyes, blinding him for a few seconds. He cleared his eyes then walked through the windy dust storm to find a taxi. But as the wind died down, a dark cloud filled the air and he noticed ahead a little wooden shack. Over the door was the words: ***Costume Shop***. It was the place in his dream. He looked around. He saw only a ghost town. He turned towards the hospital. But it had disappeared. Only cactus and tumbleweeds were seen for miles around. Then he realized: he was in that spirit world within a spirit world.

"OH, NO!" he screamed, grabbing his hair while falling to his knees. "I'm back at that ***Costume Shop***. Help me!" he cried.

The End!!!

EPILOGUE

Be aware of your surroundings when you go through this door!!!